what can(t) wait

what can(t) wait

Ashley hope Pérez

Carolrhoda LAB
MINNEAPOLIS

Carolrhoda Lab™
An imprint of Carolrhoda Books
A division of Lerner Publishing Group, Inc.
241 First Avenue North
Minneapolis, MN 55401 U.S.A.

Website address: www.lernerbooks.com

Cover and interior photographs © iStockphoto.com/Juan Estey (girl); © Amy
Nicolai/Dreamstime.com (butterfly); © Raul Touzon/National Geographic/
Getty Images (concrete).

Library of Congress Cataloging-in-Publication Data

Pérez, Ashley Hope.
        What can't wait / by Ashley Hope Pérez.
            p.   cm.
        Summary: Marooned in a broken-down Houston neighborhood—and in
    a Mexican immigrant family where making ends meet matters much more
    than making it to college—smart, talented Marisa seeks comfort elsewhere
    when her home life becomes unbearable.
        ISBN: 978–0–7613–6155–8 (trade hard cover : alk. paper)
        [1. Self-reliance—Fiction. 2. Family problems—Fiction. 3. Mexican
    Americans—Fiction.] I. Title. II. Title: What cannot wait.
    PZ7.P4255Wh 2011
    [Fic]—dc22   2010028175

Manufactured in the United States of America
1 – SB – 12/31/10

To my scholars,
for teaching me everything
about what can't wait,

y a todos los que buscan su propio camino.

November

chapter 1

You'd think that by now I'd know how to get out of the house.

Easy, right? Scrape together an outfit, make Papi and Gustavo some breakfast, grab my books, walk out the door. Finding two people camped out in the living room shouldn't change things much.

The snoring lump on the couch is my sister Cecilia, and the *niña* curled up on the couch cushions by the wall is my five-year-old niece, Anita. They show up like this whenever Cecilia has a big throw-down fight with her husband, Jose. He's definitely the bigger jerk, but I don't approve of all the screaming and door-slamming that she does in front of Anita. Or of how Cecilia drags her out of their apartment in the middle of the night, trash-talking Jose the whole time.

Cecilia is the last person that I want to deal with right now, so there are some simple rules I should follow. Don't close the bathroom door because it squeaks too loud. Wait until Cecilia is in the middle of a good long snore before slipping past. Avoid saying *anything* that sounds even remotely like "Jose" (that always stirs up the demon in her). And definitely do not stand around watching Anita sleep when I should be walking to school.

But I can't seem to help myself. Anita is the best thing that Cecilia ever did. Right now she's curled up tight as a snail and sucking both her thumbs. A tiny strip of her tan skin shows in the gap between her pink tank top and her Dora the Explorer shorts.

I smile at her, which is a mistake. Because a smile has the same effect on Anita as whispering in her ear, "Hey, someone who loves you is awake. Don't you want to get up too?"

So I've got only myself to blame when Anita's eyes pop open and she kicks free of her blanket.

"Do you got any juice, Tía Marisa?"

"What do you say?" I scoop her up and swing her into the kitchen with me.

"*Please* do you got any juice?" She kisses me on my left cheek, aiming like she always does for the ugly, thumb-sized birthmark I have there, which she says tastes like chocolate. Then she squirms away from me and starts to play hopscotch across the cracked kitchen tiles.

I pour her orange juice and set it down at the table. I'm watching her hop over when I notice a flash of something metallic between her lips.

"What's in your mouth?" I ask her.

Anita pretends not to hear and clambers onto her favorite chair, the one with the yellow seat cushion and padded back that doesn't match the others. I don't know where it came from; it just appeared one day after one of the wooden chairs broke. Anita likes it because it's the same bright yellow as a smiley face.

"Anita? Answer me."

"Don't want to tell." She picks up a paper napkin from the holder on the table and drapes it over the bottom half of her face.

"Well, you have to."

I lean closer, but Anita drops the napkin and shoots a hand up over her mouth.

"*Déjame, chica.*" I pry back her fingers as gently as I can and see silver caps on her two front teeth.

She looks like she's going to cry. "We went to the denter and he put metal on my teeth."

"The dentist? That's all?" I flick her nose. "I thought you were eating nickels for breakfast without me looking."

She giggles a little, then covers her mouth again. "My teeths is all ugly. I'm not going to smile no more."

3

"No fair, I love that smile. What if somebody tickles you?" I wrap my arms tight around her and pull her halfway up from her seat.

"*Suéltame*, Tía!" she shrieks and slaps at my hands.

I shush her, but it's too late. So much for the art of leaving.

Cecilia's up. At least her feet are. I can see them through the doorway, groping for slippers that aren't there. Time to get out.

I toss my lunch into my backpack and kiss Anita on the top of her head. "*Te quiero*. Be good, and don't eat nickels."

I slide out the back door and into the sticky Houston humidity. It's like the air in a dryer full of wet clothes. It's the Monday after Thanksgiving, but it's not even cold enough for a sweater. Right now I'd like to fall right into one of those pictures from calendars that show pretty trees with their leaves all different colors and geese flying over nice clean ponds. The scrubby yards on our street are still green, and the only sign of wildlife is a pile of dog crap in the middle of the sidewalk. I notice it just in time to step around it.

———

I'm halfway down the block before I turn and look back. Of course, there's Cecilia running up the driveway in her socks and ratty sweats. Once she sees me looking, she starts hollering my name.

God, she doesn't even have a bra on under her stained Astros shirt. I'm not all proper about things like bras, so when I say my sister needs a bra, I mean she *really* needs one. Without it, there's way more moving under there than anybody should have to face. I think about ignoring her, but I know if I don't deal with her she's going to make a scene for sure.

To give her a chance to catch up to me, I stop and pick up a Jumex juice box out of Mrs. Flores's yard and toss it into a grimy recycle bin by the curb. There, that's a good deed. If only I could be off the hook so easily.

"God, Mari," Ceci wheezes when she finally reaches me. "You didn't have to make me chase you. I don't even got my shoes on."

"Yeah, well, I've got school. What is it?" I try to sound even more irritated than I feel. With Ceci you have to lay it on thick.

Cecilia rakes a hand through her hair and lifts it off of her neck. She exhales, and I catch a whiff of something foul, like month-old burrito and seaweed. Clearly yesterday's visit to the dentist did not impress her with the importance of nighttime brushing.

"So get this," she starts in, "last night Jose waltzes in at eleven all stinking of booze and has the nerve to ask me, 'What's for dinner, *mujer?*' He knows how I hate it when he talks like that. Well, then the *cabrón* pulls out a joint and tells me I got to cook for him. Flat out like that. When it was his ass supposed to be home at seven o' clock. And then . . ."

"Hang on," I interrupt. Somewhere a lawn-mower engine starts up, sputters, then dies. "You don't have to

5

convince me he's a loser. You're the one who's still married to him. So skip to the point."

"What I'm saying is he crossed me one too many times. I mean it. Let him try to tell me to cook for him, wash his dishes! I'll break a plate over his head before I wash it for him. I . . ."

"The point, Ceci. You're making me late."

She reaches under her shirt and pulls a business card from the waistband of her sweats.

GABRIEL REYNA
ATTORNEY AT LAW
Se habla español.

8360 HOWARD DR. #26A ◆ HOUSTON, TX 77017

713-555-2020 ◆ REYNA _ LAW@LJC.COM

"See? I got an appointment at nine thirty. Help me out with Anita, OK? Just this once."

"This *once*?" I stare at her. Ceci hardly ever opens her mouth without asking me for "one more" favor.

"Yeah, just so I can figure things out."

"You expect me to skip school so I can babysit for you? Don't say another word unless you're actually planning to do something. I want to know where divorce comes in."

"*Cállate!* Somebody's going to hear!"

It's odd that Cecilia doesn't mind going outside looking the way she does, but she's suddenly paranoid about neighbors with superhuman hearing. The only person out besides us is somebody's *abuelita* rolling her trash can back up the driveway across the street, and I'm pretty sure she can't hear us over the racket the wheels make over the asphalt.

"Fine." I start walking away.

"Hang on," Cecilia says. She grabs the sleeve of my shirt. "*Mira*, the whole reason I'm asking you is because I don't want Ma to know yet. But I'm serious about it this time, *te prometo*."

"Fine, *dime*. What's your plan?"

"I'm going to find out, for real, what it would take for a divorce. So me and Anita can start over on our own."

I keep quiet, poker-faced. Ceci is probably conning me. I'm 99 percent sure that this is the case. But there's also the chance that she really might get it together and leave Jose. It's a long shot, but Jose's ten kinds of bad, and I don't want Anita to grow up like we did.

Cecilia goes in for the kill. "Just for a little while. Anita will be psyched. And you're so smart in school it don't even matter if you miss a couple hours."

"You shouldn't have left Anita alone," I say finally, turning and walking back toward the house.

"That's my sis," Cecilia says. She hurries to keep up, and her socks scuffle against the sidewalk. "No more baby money going for weed."

7

"I'll take Anita to the library until one o' clock. Then you pick us up and drop me off at school. I can't miss calculus."

"No problem, I got it."

I push open the kitchen door and toss down my backpack. Maybe I get A's in school, but I give myself an F in self-defense.

chapter 2

Over the weekend, the sign for our high school got vandalized again. Supposedly we're the Loyal Lobos, but somebody's not feeling that loyalty, because the friendly looking wolf now has a spray-painted mustache, devil horns, and an enormous penis.

"Here's your stop, *nerda*," Gustavo says. He pulls the truck over to the side of the road and throws it in park. Gustavo thinks that being my big brother exempts him from common courtesy. I don't even bother asking him to drop me off at the actual entrance.

"Damn." He sniffs and holds his nose between his grease-stained fingers. "This place stinks of all that teacher bullshit. Why show up when school's already over?"

"Don't get me started. Cecilia's fault," I say, jumping down from the truck. Ceci left me and Anita stranded at the library. After all her promises. I should have known better. I'll bet she didn't even go see the lawyer. Probably stood him up, too.

Gustavo pushes my backpack over to me. "Have fun, schoolgirl. I got to get back to the shop to finish some transmission jobs, so find a ride to work."

I slam the door.

"Don't be so serious," he calls. "Senior year, lighten up!"

I use the side entrance to get to the math hall, and I'm just about to open Ms. Ford's door when I see Alan Peralta sitting on the stairs a little farther down the hall. He has his head bowed over his sketchbook, and his shaggy brown hair hangs across his forehead. His lips are parted the tiniest bit, and a little pink triangle of tongue peeks out at the corner of his mouth.

He looks up and catches me staring.

"Hey," he says. He flips the sketchbook closed, caps his Sharpie, and stands up. He's about 5'11", no giant, but tall for a Hispanic guy. We were in homeroom together freshman year, and I'm pretty sure we were the same height back then. Now I don't even come up to his nose.

He walks over to me, looking delicious in a gray T-shirt and khaki cargo pants. "Brenda said you were stopping by here. I thought you might want the econ notes." He fishes around in his bag and pulls out a sheet of paper.

"You mean Mrs. T. actually taught today?" I move closer, but I keep my head tilted just the slightest bit so that my birthmark is on the side away from him.

"Crazy, I know. Don't worry, she only lasted about fifteen minutes, then she was back surfing the Internet. But she said this stuff would be on the quiz." He shows me the notes, which only take up half of the page. The rest is covered by an ink drawing of a fanged wolf swinging a baseball bat. "Sorry about that. I've been trying to come up with a design for the team's new spirit T-shirts. Jimmy's been on my ass about it."

"Drawback of having your brother as your coach, I guess. It looks good. You sure you don't need to keep it?"

Alan taps his sketchbook. "I've got another one in here. That one was just a warm-up."

His hand is so close to mine when he gives me the notes. Brenda would tell me to just grow some balls and touch his hand to show some interest. She'd finesse this moment, no problem. But I take the notes by the corner of the page, like he's got leprosy or something.

"I'll give them back in the morning, maybe before first period? In the cafeteria?"

He nods but doesn't move. I hope he doesn't think I'm trying to invite myself to his breakfast table.

His big hands toy with the worn cover of his sketch-book while I search for something else to say. It's cool that you thought of me? You're a great artist? You've sure *changed* since freshman year?

11

"Got to grab my calculus homework. It's pretty terminal to miss Ms. Ford's class." Brilliant.

I cut my losses and duck into the classroom.

———

The problems are tough, but all I have to do to keep motivated is think of what my dad said when I told him and Ma that I signed up for AP calculus. "Girls and numbers don't mix, *mija*. Leave the mathematics to the men." Total bullshit. He'll see when I pass the exam.

I'm packing up when Ms. Ford calls me over. Her glasses are always sliding down the bridge of her nose, and her blonde hair is half in, half out of its barrette. I hope she's not going to say something embarrassing about "family problems."

She shuffles through a mess of papers and hands me an envelope that says "The University of Texas" and, in smaller letters, "Recommendation for Ms. Marisa Moreno."

I run my fingers over the letters and imagine a different envelope coming for me. I'll pull out a letter and read, "Congratulations, Ms. Moreno! We are delighted to invite you to join our freshman class in the School of Engineering. . . ."

But then reality takes a bite out of my little fantasy and leaves me remembering what happened when I told my parents that with my GPA and SAT scores I qualified for automatic admission to the University of Houston. My mom got up to throw another tortilla on the *comal*.

My dad pointed his fork at me and said, "It's only because some *gringos* want to feel good about themselves, want to feel like they're helping out some poor *mexicana*. Don't think that gets you out of working."

And that was only talking about a college right here in Houston. Ever since I wrote "Engineering" as my career goal on some survey from the first day of school, Ms. Ford hasn't stopped telling me how great UT–Austin is. World-class engineering program, amazing libraries, research opportunities with top faculty, big scholarships.

The truth is that I just picked engineering because it sounded good, better than being a nurse's assistant or working at SuperCuts. I mean, engineers use lots of math and work in air-conditioning, right? That's all I need to know for now. Sometimes Ms. Ford starts talking about civil, mechanical, and electrical engineering, but she might as well be talking about her three favorite poodle breeds for all it means to me.

If you put me in a world where all that matters is what I want, I'd go to UT and give engineering a shot. But that is definitely not my world. I can't just peace-out on my family. If I repeated Ms. Ford's ooh-la-la UT list to my mother, the words would hit her and bounce right off like rubber arrows. There's no way they can penetrate the fortress of *familia*.

"You finished the essay?" Ms. Ford asks, holding somebody's homework up in front of her mouth because she's still chewing an Oreo from the package she always has on her desk. She's always eating something.

I want to say, What's the point, miss? But since Ms. Ford is seriously lacking in knowledge about Mexican families, I just say, "Not yet."

Ms. Ford frowns down at her calendar. "Application deadline is coming up. I want to see an essay from you on Friday." She pulls out her tutorial schedule. "How about bringing it by right after school?"

She's writing down the appointment in blue crayon before I even respond. She can never find a pen when she needs it.

"Fine, I'll write the essay."

"Of course you will," Ms. Ford says. "Oreo?"

The fight in me is all used up, so I take one.

———

The cafeteria is mostly empty, and I spot Brenda right away. Next to her, some white guy I don't recognize is playing a guitar. She's laughing and leaning against the far wall, which is just one huge, greasy window that faces a scrubby courtyard with picnic tables. The afternoon light angling in behind her gives her a sort of glow, like La Virgen de Guadalupe in a church painting. But this is all show. Brenda is so not the virgin in our friendship.

Most of the time I'm fine with how I look. Average build, average boobs, average brown eyes, broad Mexican nose, and black hair. Whatever. But when I walk toward Brenda, I suddenly feel awkward and embarrassed to be wearing my polo shirt for work and no makeup. One look at her and you'd know what I mean. Brenda has perfect caramel skin and these big eyes, plus a delicate little nose and a smile like she's already got you figured out. Then there's her body. Picture the Latina Barbie doll minus the plastic and ugly clothes, and you're on the right track.

The guy with Brenda has his head bent over the guitar, and I think maybe she has finally met her match. This guy is hot. His body is seriously built under that white T-shirt and jeans, and his face is straight out of an Abercrombie ad. He's laughing when I walk up. His blond eyebrows shoot up, and he tilts his head back. Even his Adam's apple is sexy. I don't blame Brenda for not noticing me until I'm right in front of them.

"Marisa!" Brenda throws her arms around me like she hasn't seen me in a week. She doesn't give me a chance to say anything before she's pulling me closer to the guy. "Hey, this is Greg; he just transferred from Lamar. Greg, this is Marisa, my best friend since forever." He grins, and I think he's already in love with everything about Brenda, right down to the way she says his name with a touch of an accent. He leans the guitar against the window and sticks out his hand for me to shake.

"Hey Marisa," he says. "Nice to meet you."

He surprises me by getting my name right on the first try. A lot of white people say my name all ugly and flat, with an "uh" at the end.

"Greg's got U.S. Government with us," Brenda says. "I promised Dominguez I'd help him catch up."

"Lucky Greg," I say, rolling my eyes.

Greg just nods and says, "Yep, lucky me." He's still smiling.

I stick my phone in Brenda's face to show her the time. She reluctantly detaches herself from Greg, but not before she adds his phone number to her cell and gets him to promise to show her how to play something on his guitar tomorrow. Brenda has this way of making things happen. Me, I just stand around fantasizing about touching Alan's hand.

She shoots Greg a few sexy looks over her shoulder as we walk away. "Dominguez really did ask me to show him around, no lie."

"Yeah, that's noble of you. What a sacrifice."

"Well, he's going to need some help, you know, to fit in. What is he, like the sixth white guy in the whole damn school?"

Whatever, *güerita*. You'll make him feel right at home. You're every white boy's secret fantasy."

Brenda's hands go right to her hips. "Hey, just because I got green contacts don't make me *güera*. I'm as Mexican as I am Cuban, and plenty proud of *mi cultura*."

"*No te creas*; I'm just kidding," I say fast. "But maybe I should warn Gringo Greg about your man-eating past."

"Be careful, I *am* your ride," she says. As if she'd leave me behind. But she does change the subject. "Seriously, what is Ceci's problem? *Qué pendeja*. When you were texting me today, I almost got my phone taken up in English because I started cussing at it. Thank God I'm an only child. I mean, to just leave you stranded at the library, and after she promised!"

"Oh, it gets better. The dentist told her a while ago not to give Anita milk at night before bed, but of course she didn't listen. So Anita's front teeth got really bad and they had to put silver caps on. I guess Jose said something about how they look, and now Anita's too embarrassed to smile. She wouldn't even let me read her funny books at the library, and she puts her hand up in front of her mouth when she's talking."

A bunch of guys from the basketball team are hanging out just inside the gym as we go by. LeRoy catches sight of Brenda and steps into the doorway. "Looking fine, Bren," he says. "Where you been?" He's trying to play it cool, but he's fidgeting with the basketball in his hands and he grins at Brenda way too long. Desperate's the word.

"Can you play with that thing in?" she asks, pointing at his mouth. Brenda's interest in LeRoy lasted about five minutes—and it ended about the same time he got himself fitted with a gold grill studded with rhinestones.

Brenda doesn't give him a chance to respond. "See you, LeRoy," she says, shoving him playfully back toward the gym before she grabs my arm and tugs me on toward the door.

"God, too much BET or what? I cannot get past the grill," Brenda says once we're outside.

"Well, I remember when you were talking about what beautiful caramel-colored kids you guys could have someday. . . ."

"Shut up, that was ages ago."

"Try two months ago."

"Maybe," Brenda says all serious, "we should take some pictures of LeRoy's grill and tell Anita that some people put metal on their teeth to be cool. Think that'd make her feel better?"

I laugh. "Can't you just hear her? 'Teeth jewelry, Tía!' Then she'll want diamonds."

"Speaking of diamonds, a certain second baseman was looking for you today."

"Yeah, I know. I saw him."

"You're smiling!" Her voice is singsong.

"He just gave me our econ notes," I say. "That was it." Brenda is not exactly subtle about these things, and I don't want to give her any new ammunition.

"How *muy, muy* thoughtful," she says and elbows me. "Just say the word and you've got Cupid Zepeda at your service."

chapter 3

I hold the back door open for my mom. We're both yawning, and as soon as she gets inside, she kicks off her shoes and drops into a chair. "Another day finished, *gracias a Dios*," she says. I grab the lotion from the counter and sit down next to her. I have to massage her feet because by this time of night her hands hurt too much to do it. She's been working at the bakery forever, and all the kneading she does with dough turns her arthritis murderous. Her feet swell up bad from standing so long, and I stare at the floor while I rub them so I won't have to see them all puffy and twisted.

There's a crash in the living room.

"Boo!" Anita shouts as she jumps into the kitchen. She drops on all fours and scoots across the floor on the knees of her pajamas.

"I thought I smelled a rat!" I wipe my hands on a napkin and reach out for a hug.

"Just a little *ratón*." Anita covers the two silver teeth with her tongue and wriggles her fingers from her cheeks like whiskers.

"What are you doing still awake, *mija*?" Mami asks her. "*Ya es muy tarde*." She can't stand to see Anita run loose. Plus, if she wakes up my dad, there'll be hell to pay.

Anita runs to the door, picks up the shoes from where Ma dropped them, and places them neatly against the wall.

"I been helping my mommy," she tells me. "Can I help Abuelita too?"

"Ask her. You know how."

"Abue, *¿Puedo ayudarte en algo?*" Anita asks in her shy Spanish.

"*No, gracias. Vete a dormir, mija*." Ma waves her away, but not before she pulls down the hand that Anita has over her mouth.

"I'll put her to bed," I say. "Come on, little *ratón*."

"Mommy's getting pretty," Anita whispers as I steer her toward the living room.

"Oh really?" I know what's up as soon as I see the stupid bouquet of flowers on the coffee table. They're pink roses, Cecilia's favorite. They already look a little brown at the edges, and I can just see Jose picking them up from the "Reduced for Quick Sale" table in the Wal-Mart floral section. Here we go.

I turn out the living room lights and settle Anita in her little corner sleeping spot.

"Paco?" Anita looks around for my old teddy bear. Paco was Cecilia's first, then Gustavo's, and then mine. Now he gets a good dose of Anita whenever she's here.

"Hang on, *chiquita*." I find Paco in the hall. He has two hair clips attached to his ears like earrings. The bathroom door is open a little, and I can see a slice of Cecilia's hand holding a mascara wand.

I carry the teddy bear back to the living room, tuck him into the covers with Anita, and stroke her hair until she falls asleep.

***

"Hey," Cecilia says when I push the bathroom door open. She doesn't look away from her reflection.

"*¿Qué haces?*" I ask.

"Just spoiling myself a little." She streaks eyeliner under her left eye.

"Do you have anything to say to me?"

"Oh yeah. Sorry about earlier. I got caught up and . . ."

"Cut the crap. Did you talk to the lawyer?"

"Maybe," she says. She sucks in her breath to find her cheekbones and dusts them pink. She looks totally uninterested in what I just said.

"*Hello?*" I wave a hand between Cecilia and the mirror. "What are you going to do?"

She shrugs. "Jose's going to stop by on his way home from work."

"So what are you going to say? What about the div—"

"Shut up!" she snaps. "It's my business, *entiendes*? Jose and me just got crossways is all. He already called and said he was sorry. He means it; I know he does."

"I bet. And he also said he's going to help around the house and stop boozing during the week and quit smoking pot?"

Cecilia shoots me a look. "I never said he was perfect. But he wants me to go back to school. He's going to work more hours so that when Anita starts kindergarten we'll have money for me to do a cosmetology program."

"You can do that without him, Ceci. You know you can. Don't put Anita through this again. She's not a baby. She's too big for you to just stick her in her room like nothing is happening while you two are going at each other."

"You think you know everything, don't you?" Cecilia's eyes narrow. "One day maybe you'll have your own fucking *problemas* to worry about. Then we'll see who's so smart."

"You've got a lot of nerve. A shitload of nerve." I walk out of the bathroom so mad I'm shaking.

"Yeah, well, *es mi vida*!" Cecilia says. "Get your own!"

chapter 4

I don't know how to swim, and I'm lost deep in muddy water. Seaweed fingers wrap themselves in my hair. The shadows of slippery things I can't see circle over me. I know I'm running out of air, but I can't get to the surface. My head feels heavy, and . . .

5:00 A.M. My alarm clock flashes red and starts blaring Shakira and static. Usually I slap it off right away, but today it takes me longer to get free of the dream.

"Marisa!" Papi shouts. "*Calla la maldita alarma!*" He pounds the wall that separates our bedrooms until I get my hands on the alarm clock and turn it off.

The dream sticks with me, making shadows in the back of my brain while I get dressed and wash my face. I carry my backpack to the kitchen and think how empty the living room seems. Three days was all it took for me to get used to having Anita around, but now she and Cecilia are back with Jose.

In the kitchen, my report card is in the same place I left it yesterday, untouched. I've been doing this since middle school, hoping that one day my parents will say something. If I stick the grades right in my mom's face, she says, "*Qué bueno*," but I don't think the A's even register to her. I grab the report card and toss it in the drawer with all the others that they've ignored. Then I get to work.

I'm almost done with my calculus homework when Papi comes into the kitchen trailing a steamy soap smell.

For a second I consider finishing the last few lines of the problem, but I know better. I close the book.

"*Buenos días*, Papi. You want eggs?"

"*Con chile y tocino*," he says without looking at me.

I throw extra bacon into the skillet because I can hear Gustavo in the shower. Mami sleeps in after her late nights at the bakery, but Gustavo always expects breakfast.

My dad pulls out his supplies from the pantry and sets his work boots on the floor by his chair. I listen for him to start polishing them, but he doesn't make a sound. When I crack the last egg into a bowl, I turn and see Papi staring at my calculus book and pencil.

"*Mueva esas cosas*," he says. His voice is sharp.

"OK, Papi." I move my things off of the table, but I don't apologize.

I'm relieved when he starts to polish his work boots like he does every day. Now he'll be too busy to get mad at me. He dabs cleaner on any muddy places and massages the dirt out. Then he rubs on a sealer to protect the leather. The last step is a careful buff with a wadded sheet of newspaper.

My mom says Papi makes such a big deal about his boots because he didn't get his first pair of real shoes until he was thirteen. Then she always reminds me of how bad life was for him in Mexico and how I should remember that I'm an American citizen because of his hard work.

I wait until my dad finishes with his boots before I set the plate in front of him. Keeping the peace is all about doing what Papi wants when he wants it.

I clean up the kitchen and listen to his fork scrape on the plate. I don't have to look to know that he is sitting perfectly straight, like Mami taught us to sit in church. But it looks to me like it hurts Papi to sit that way. Plus there's this sunken look to his cheeks like he never gets enough to eat, even though I cook for him all the time.

My dad's fork clatters against his plate.

"Something else, Papi?"

He shakes his head, hands me the dish, and walks out without a word.

"Love you, too," I say to the empty room. "Have a great day."

When I see a roach climb into the box with Papi's boot-cleaning supplies, I don't chase it down.

chapter 5

It's Friday afternoon, and I probably would have skipped all the way to Ms. Ford's room if the halls were empty. Because I actually wrote the UT application essay, and I think it might even be OK.

This is a semi-miracle because I hate essays. Despise them. My English teacher, Mrs. Garza, always talks about how writing should open up your world, that there are no wrong answers. But essays are always asking you to put yourself in little boxes, to make yourself fit in three to five pages. "Describe the person you most admire" really means: Are you the kind of person who admires

    (a) a relative

    (b) a famous person/celebrity/role model

    (c) some random person for a reason you can't explain?

There are *definitely* wrong answers.

UT wanted me to "Describe a significant setback, challenge, or opportunity in your life and the impact that it has had on you." I worried about that a lot, because you're supposed to show how something hard ended up teaching you a lesson. But what about things that are just hard without being good for you? I can't just make up some pretty story about how coming from Mexico was difficult for my parents, and education is now the number-one priority in our house. Maybe that's true in Lifetime movies, but not in my house.

I had to do something to get started, so I decided to just write down everything I knew I couldn't put in my essay.

—————

Dear UT,

My sister got pregnant at seventeen, giving up her career at Sonic to take care of the baby and hate her husband Jose full time. My brother has a GED, and his idea of a long-term goal is saving up money to get new rims for his truck. My parents are not interested in learning English—they only took that one class so that they could meet the requirements to get citizenship. Papi loves my paycheck and only tolerates me, and Mami's biggest dream is for me to get married and live in a house on this same street so that she can watch her *nietos* grow up just as unhappy. Oh, and if

you're wondering why I missed the PSAT last year when I should have tried for National Merit Scholar, it was because no one else could stay home to watch my niece that day.

———————

I know that sounds pissy and super-critical, but it's completely true. Then it hit me that I feel this way because I know I want something different. And all of a sudden I got the feeling that I might actually be able to write an essay about that. I crossed out my list of complaints and started again.

Now Ms. Ford is reading the essay, and I'm watching her face. She stops a couple of times to scratch down notes on the backside of one of her handouts. I can't even read them because she's writing with a dry-erase marker. I offer her my pencil, but she waves it away.

When she looks up, she's smiling. She goes over a few things with me—be more specific here, you get a little off track there, check the spelling of the circled words—then she hands me my paper.

"All you need is a conclusion," she says, stretching her arms over her head.

"But didn't I already…"

"You're almost there. You show how they don't understand what you want to do. Now show what, exactly, you want to be different in your life and how UT fits into that."

I think about that for a minute before I start writing. I mark a bunch of things out, add some new things, rewrite it, then take it up to Ms. Ford's desk.

I watch the life that my parents lead, and I know that I want something different. They have worked hard their entire lives with no savings to show for it. My dad dropped out of school in Mexico before third grade; my mom "graduated" from middle school. My brother and sister got out of high school, but they don't want anything more.

I want my hard work to get me somewhere. I want to worry about which engineering firm to work for, not how I'm going to pay the light bill.

So why do I make my life so hard? Because I want to make something of myself. Because I want my mom to look at me in ten years and finally understand why a high school diploma wasn't enough for me.

"You got it," Ms. Ford says. "Just clean this baby up, type it, and send the application in."

I don't want Ms. Ford to get the idea that I'm excited about UT, but I can't stop myself from grinning. I start to imagine myself at UT. It's easy because I've practically got all the "student life" photos from the website memorized. There I am, sitting in the front of a big lecture hall with my pen out and notebook ready. Or waving from a desk on the top floor of the gigantic main library. I could be standing around a dorm microwave with three other girls, all of us eating ramen noodles . . .

There's a bunch of shouting in the hall, and I look up to see two freshman guys scrambling to hold Ms. Ford's door open for Brenda. She walks in with her arms full of stuffed animals. One of them falls as she dumps the heap onto a desk.

"What are those?" I'm laughing before I even get the words out.

"What do they look like? Christmas Gobblers. It's our next fund-raiser for nursing club." Brenda picks up one of the plush turkeys and shakes it. "Isn't he cute?"

"Definitely original," Ms. Ford says.

"I think of turkeys as going more with Thanksgiving," I say.

"Uh, no! See? He's got a green-and-red sweater and everything."

"I can see it." Ms. Ford squints and turns to lower the blinds behind her. She's trying to hide a smile. "Like Frosty the Snow Turkey."

Brenda rolls her eyes. "Very funny, miss."

It looks to me like the retailer didn't quite unload all of their autumn merchandise. "Did you get them on sale?" I ask.

"Maybe," Brenda says, which means yes. "Let's just hope the freshmen buy thousands of them. You want a ride to work or what?"

I gobble at her. "That's 'please' in turkey."

"See, you like them so much I'll tell Alan he should buy you one."

That shuts me up.

"Grab some of these for me, will you?" she says. "Just don't bend the tags."

I say good-bye to Ms. Ford and scoop up a dozen of the turkeys. We're halfway down the hall when Ms. Ford walks out and calls, "I want to see your essay before you send it all in."

"Yeah, OK," I mumble. My cheeks start to burn.

Brenda looks at me hard. "I thought U of H didn't have an essay."

"Ms. Ford's been ragging me about applying to UT–Austin. I mean, it just got easier to actually do the application than to listen to her. No biggie, just an idea."

"I know about your ideas, Marisa. When were you going to tell me?" Brenda grips her armful of turkeys tighter, bending up some of the tags.

"There's nothing to tell, I just . . ."

"Well, shit, forget it!" Brenda spins around and starts walking fast. I try to help her when she stumbles in her high heels, but she just pushes through the doors to the student parking lot. A few steps later, a turkey tumbles from her arms and lands in the gutter. She still doesn't stop. I pick up the turkey and brush it off.

Brenda crushes a few more tags trying to get her keys out. Finally she lets me help, but she still won't look at me.

We dump the gobblers into the backseat. "Look," she says finally, "you're too smart for community college, *eso ya sé*, and that's OK. But what's wrong with U of H? I thought we were going to stick together here in Houston. Like always."

"We will stick together. I just . . ."

"*No importa.*" She yanks her car door closed. "Really. I'm just surprised, that's all." She stares straight ahead, fumbles with the keys, and starts the car.

"Don't be mad," I say.

"I'm not mad."

Brenda backs up without looking. The driver behind her honks, and she shoots him the finger.

"I just thought I'd be at junior college and you'd be at U of H and we'd do our homework at Burger King or the *taquería*. We'd hang out, and you'd finally really start going out and everything. I thought you wanted that too." Brenda's knuckles are white on the steering wheel.

"I do want it," I say, but I know she's not buying it.

This is how stubborn Brenda is. We both know that the plans we made in middle school don't have anything to do with the way the world really is. We said crazy stuff like how we'd start college together and hit up the parties, but also get good grades. Go on double dates and meet handsome guys who are best friends. Finish college and get good jobs. Get married and buy big houses next door to each other, and then two years later have babies at the same time and be *comadres*. Watch our kids grow up best friends.

When we were younger, I imagined that finishing high school would be like waving a magic wand, and then my dad would like me and Ma would understand me and Ceci wouldn't dump on me and Gustavo would do the dishes for once and I'd have my own life.

But here I am, seventeen years old and still tiptoeing around my dad, trying to please my mom, getting bulldozed by Cecilia and ignored by Gustavo. In Brenda's house, she's the princess, so it's different for her. But what I want doesn't matter.

"Nothing makes sense anymore," I say.

Brenda turns up the radio.

chapter 6

Lucky for me, Brenda doesn't stay mad that long. After two days of bumming rides from other people, I see her waiting for me in the hall when school lets out. I glance down to make sure the sealed UT application envelope is still sandwiched out of sight between my calculus book and my binder.

"Want to get a burger and hang out before work?" she asks.

This is Brenda's way of saying sorry, so I agree. Since I don't start work until a little later today, we drive through Jack in the Box and then go to Brenda's.

Brenda is decking out her burger with jalapeños and I'm spooning salsa onto mine when the back door opens and her mom comes in with her arms full of construction paper and that weird gray-brown, recycled paper with dashed lines that they always made us use in elementary school. "Hey girls," she says. She swoops in for a kiss from Brenda and then comes over to the counter where I'm screwing the lid onto the salsa jar.

"Life, how is it?" she asks me.

"Good, Ms. Zepeda, thanks," I say.

"You two can help me grade if you want. All you got to do is check that they wrote three sentences and that the picture's got something to do with what they put down."

"Ugh, Mom, no way!" Brenda says, rolling her eyes. "We were just about to go do homework, you know." She grabs the salsa and swings open the fridge door. I get a good look at Brenda's grades—four B's, one A, and a C—there's a sticky note with a smiley face and the words, "Hard worker!" in bubbly letters stuck to the front. That's the kind of reception you get when your mom's a third-grade teacher, I guess.

By the time we get to the mom-free zone of Brenda's room, I can tell she's dying to dish about Greg. That's fine by me, just so long as she isn't pissed anymore.

"So he invited me to ride around with him later. His dad has a Tahoe, how cool is that?"

"Mmmm-ummm," I say through a mouthful of fries. I wash them down with a swig of Brenda's Coke.

She gets back at me by snatching a huge handful of my fries.

"Hey!" I swat her hand away, but I'm too late. "So what's his story? Where's he live?"

"Used to live with his dad downtown, but he got fed up with Lamar. It's all preppy like people say it is, you know, all academic and shit. Too stressful. So he moved in with his mom. She has one of those nice apartments on Meadowbrook."

"You already saw his apartment?"

"Oh yeah," she says. She carriers her burger over to the bed, closes her eyes, and stretches. Her face says GUILTY x 40.

I wad up one of her shirts from the floor and throw it at her. "You're so bad, girl," I say, because that's what I always say. But I don't worry too much, because I dragged her sexy self to Planned Parenthood sophomore year.

Brenda stares at her fingernails and picks at her cuticle a little, no doubt reliving some delicious moment with Greg. "Maybe, but being bad feels so good. You know what I mean."

The thing is, I don't. Although lately I have been imagining in some detail what it'd be like to snuggle up to a certain baseball player in my economics class.

"You can't fool me, Marisa Moreno," Brenda says, pointing a fry at me. "*No lo niegues* because I know you like I know my bra size. You and Alan Peralta are getting nice and close."

"Yeah, right. I wish."

"He's totally in love with you. From what I can tell, he has been since freshman year. You just need to . . ."

"Alan? We're friends and everything, but he's way out of my league."

"Then why hasn't he been dating other girls?"

"He's got baseball and his drawing. Plus that job at his brother's restaurant."

Brenda throws up her hands. "Don't be *tonta*. You heard it here first. When have I ever been wrong? I have a sense about these things."

I'm about to remind her about LeRoy—and all the other guys she's "loved" before Greg—when my phone rings.

"That's probably Alan," Brenda says, looking proud of herself.

But it's Cecilia.

"Marisa?" she says, voice shaking. "You got to help me."

I roll my eyes at Brenda and mouth "Cecilia." She probably wants me to babysit Anita so she can go get her nails done.

But I'm way off.

"Somebody just called from the Ben Taub E.R. It's Jose. They wouldn't tell me what; they wouldn't tell me anything. They just said not to come alone."

"What? Was he working?"

"Some construction job on the west side, he just started last week. I don't know where . . . I don't know . . ." Her voice cracks.

"Calm down, Ceci. You don't want to scare Anita."

"I just took her next door to Mrs. Salinas. Shit, Mari. I'm so scared."

"Just hang in there. I'm coming." Brenda hears the weirdness in my voice and is already off the bed and throwing stuff in her purse. "I'm going to get Brenda to bring me over, then I can drive with you to the hospital, OK?"

"Hurry," Cecilia whispers.

———

All that the nurses in the emergency room will tell us is that there was an accident, Jose is being cared for, and the doctor is on his way to explain the details. It must have been a long walk, because I have time to call at least a dozen people before he finally shows up.

The doctor is a small man in crumpled blue scrubs and white sneakers. He has a funny name full of consonants. I forget it as soon as he says it.

"Who is the wife of Mr. Jose Almaguer?"

Cecilia lifts her hand.

"I see," he says and turns toward her. "Your husband has been in a serious accident. He is fortunate to be alive."

Cecilia slips down a little in her chair.

"Your husband was on a work site, he was using a fork-lift, and . . ."

Dr. Unpronounceable presses his lips together like he's trying to decide if Cecilia can handle this. I grip her hand. He still doesn't say anything, and I'm ready to scream.

"And?" I ask, trying to sound calm.

"It seems that somehow Jose was separated from the machine he was operating." He consults his clipboard and glances up at Cecilia. "He fell down in front of the forklift, it continued to move forward at a high speed, and the result was that he was crushed against a wall. Both legs are fractured in many places, and his right hipbone was completely shattered."

Cecilia dissolves into tears. I rub her back and watch the doctor angle his fingers into a bridge in the air. He's brown like us, but probably Indian. His voice sounds so crisp and proper, the kind of British English that belongs with fancy teacups and rose gardens, not here with antiseptic cleaner and broken bones and blood.

He picks up his clipboard again, glances over the notes scribbled on the front page. "Your husband will be in surgery for several more hours as we pin the broken leg bones together. We will also need to remove bone shards from the hip area and check for internal bleeding in the nearby organs."

"What happens after that?" I ask.

"We won't know until later how much permanent damage has been done to his body. His face may need some minor reconstruction, but the wounds there are mostly superficial. But if, for example, a bone was forced into the spinal cord, there is a chance of paralysis. Or . . ."

"Thank you," I cut in before he can scare Cecilia even more. "We'll wait to hear more after the surgery."

The doctor nods, shakes our hands, and says he'll notify us of any developments. Then he's gone.

Cecilia doesn't move. Her eyes are glassy, and her chin wobbles. "I don't know what to do," she whispers.

"We just have to wait," I say. "Mami will be here as soon as someone can pick her up. I can go get her now if you want."

"No," she says. "I mean, you tried to tell me. I should have gotten out while I could. *Pero esto cambia todo.* What if Jose can't work again, what if he's hurt for good and . . ." She trails off.

"Try not to worry. It'll be OK." But all I'm thinking is, *oh shit.*

chapter 7

Hours drip by. I stop looking at my watch and measure the time by how tired the doctor looks. He keeps coming in with updates that blur together. They pinned his right leg together.... They started the left.... Pieces of his shattered hip were extracted.... Some internal bleeding in his lower abdomen, another surgery for that....

I know it's been a long time because when he comes in to tell us that last bit, the doctor's mustache is drooping and there's a shadow of stubble on his cheeks that wasn't there earlier.

The waiting room fills up with people, but nearly everybody is related to Jose. I recognize his parents and older sisters from the wedding and Anita's birthday parties, and I can see enough resemblance in the half dozen other people around them to know that they're part of the same gene pool. I recognize Pedro Jimenez, one of Jose's cousins who also happens to be in my graduating class. I give him a little wave, but he doesn't see me. Maybe he doesn't even know who I am. He doesn't spend that much time at school, anyway.

Across the room there's a girl about my age with her family. They stick out because they're white in the sea of brown. Whatever their emergency is, I can just tell by how the girl slides her phone open, grins, and starts texting that it's not exactly hitting her in the gut. Who knows, maybe her brother-in-law just got himself smashed up on the job, too. But her parents are there, the dad in a business suit, the mom in a pretty gray dress, all hushed voices and serious looks. Now the girl is up out of her seat, and her mom gives her a hug and hands her a wad of bills. She slips the money into her jeans pocket, pulls her T-shirt down over her flat tummy, and strolls out of the waiting room. Just like that, so easy.

Me, I haven't left the room except to pee since we got here, because right now I'm all Cecilia's got. My mom is still waiting for someone to pick her up from the bakery. When I tried to leave to go get her, Ceci started to cry all over again. I mention it again now, but she doesn't want to be left alone. So I call Gustavo's cell and Papi's work like every five minutes. I still can't get them.

I'm just about to text Brenda to take her up on her offer to get Mami when my mom walks in. I squeeze Cecilia's hand, and then I see that Alan is right behind her. He's in a damp T-shirt and Nike shorts, like he just came from the gym, and for just a moment I forget all about Jose.

Within seconds Cecilia is hanging on my mom's neck and crying into her hair. Mami hustles her off to the bathroom so they can be in private. That leaves me to come up with something to say to Alan.

"Thanks, I . . . how'd you know? I mean . . ."

"Brenda called me. Your mom's bakery's really close to the gym where me and Jimmy work out. It was no problem."

An intercom from the nurse's station blares a doctor's name, and we both sort of jump.

"Gustavo should have picked her up, it's just he won't answer his phone. My dad ought to be coming, too, but . . ." I look around, like maybe the irresponsible men in my family are here, just hiding behind the table stacked with boxes of Crystal Flake doughnuts and everything else people brought. Because whatever our other failings, Mexicans don't let people in a crisis go hungry.

"No problem, really." Alan just smiles at me.

"Well, thanks again," I say. I can feel myself blushing, and I fight the urge to put my hand over my birthmark. I figure he can't wait to get out of here, probably just brought Ma as a favor to Brenda.

"You want some company?"

I manage to smile, and a minute later we're sitting together on the hard plastic chairs.

"It's packed in here," I say. Queen of the obvious, that's me.

"Looks like La Raza is having its meeting at Ben Taub tonight," Alan says, all calm and serious-looking.

When I explode into giggles, two ladies praying the rosary in the corner stare daggers at me. I want to hide.

"So what happened, exactly?" he says, leaning forward so that no one can hear us.

"My sister's husband is not the smartest," I whisper, shooting a glance at his family along the other wall. "Take any situation, right, and he'll do the one stupidest, most dangerous thing a person can do. And he works construction—really bad idea. Somehow he fell off a running forklift and ended up in between it and a wall."

"Ouch. How's your sister?"

"Well, you saw. She's pretty worked up. Whatever they're doing is going to cost a fortune. No insurance, of course." I lower my voice even more. "Jose's always been trouble, and Cecilia was actually talking divorce just a week ago. But she won't leave him now since he's all smashed up. She practically said as much to me."

Just then Cecilia and my mom walk over. Cecilia's not crying anymore, and she forces a smile.

"Thanks," she says to Alan.

He offers Mami his chair, but she motions for him to sit back down.

"*No te preocupes*; I have a seat over there," my mom says, pointing to where the rosary ladies are.

"I'm so glad you're here, Mami." I kiss her on the cheek and hug her.

"A *buen hombre*, this one," she says, patting Alan's shoulder. "*Dios sabe* where Gustavo is, that *malcriado* who thinks the car shop is his family. He should be here." She crosses herself. "We can only pray."

The doctor comes over to give Cecilia the latest update. There's probably no paralysis, but Jose will be stuck in bed for a long time, and he's going to need lots of physical therapy just to walk again. The doctor doesn't meet Cecilia's eyes when he tells her that Jose will have serious back and leg problems for the rest of his life and will no longer be able to do any kind of physical labor.

Cecilia takes it more calmly than I expect. When she walks over to her mother-in-law, all I want to do is keep talking to Alan. OK, if I'm honest with myself, what I want to do is touch his arm, put my head on his shoulder, and breathe in his smell of soap and sweat. But I look up and see Mami watching me. She lifts her rosary when she catches my eye.

This makes me want to scream because already I'm getting up. I'm going to go over there just like she expects me to. I've seen Brenda blow off her mom a million times, but between me and even the smallest rebellion there's this huge pit that I have no idea how to cross.

I apologize to Alan and join my mother like the good daughter I'm supposed to be.

———

Jose is still unconscious when Cecilia, Mami, and I finally get to see him. His face is bruised all over, patches of it dark purple. I can see brown shadows of his blood under the bandage across his left cheek. His legs are in white casts, and he's hooked into some kind of crazy elevation machine.

At first no one says anything. Then Cecilia drops her wadded Kleenex and starts choking out a new round of sobs. We wrap our arms around her. She shakes right there between us for a long time.

Then I hear footsteps in the hall. My dad's standing in the doorway, stiff and serious like always. Gustavo's right behind him. Both of them are still in work clothes, sweaty and smeared with grease. I'd like to ask where the hell they've been, but I don't.

"*Mija*," Papi says. He stares at Jose's hospital bed. Finally he walks closer to us. He puts a hand on Ceci's arm. This is as close as my father gets to hugs. "*Vamos a ayudarte*," he says.

But then his arms cross back over his chest, and the words hang cold and formal in the air, less a reassurance than an accusation. It's like he's saying, *we'll help you, but not because you deserve it.*

"*Sí, cariño*, we're gonna help you," Mami repeats more gently.

As much as I'm sorry for what's happened to Jose and what it's going to mean for Ceci, the person I'm most worried about is myself. It doesn't make me proud, but I can already see what's coming. I know from the looks on my parents' faces that this *we* they're talking about is really going to be a lot of *me*. Whether I like it or not, helping Ceci just got bumped to obligation number one in my life. Because when your sister's in trouble—real trouble—you don't get to walk away.

December

chapter 8

I'm at Kroger in my smile-and-scan cashier mode. The customer at my register is buying about four hundred cans of Fancy Feast cat food. No joke. This is the kind of thing the other cashiers complain about, but I don't mind. The cans pass through my hands, and the *bleep, bleep, bleep* of the scanner fades into background noise. The only problem is that, before I realize it, the rhythm's tricked my mind into thinking it can go wherever it wants, and it slides back to how things at home have turned to shit.

Obviously Jose can't work, and it's near impossible for a day laborer with no contract to collect workers' compensation. So now Ceci works a ten-hour day at a gas station, and I have Anita to take care of until she gets off from work and whenever she has to take Jose for special medical appointments. Plus I still have my shifts at Kroger.

It would all be easier to take if Jose had been mugged, hurt in a car accident, sick with some rare disease, anything besides the misfortune of his own stupidity. Here's how he got himself smashed up: (1) He lied to the foreman and said he knew how to use a forklift. (2) He left the forklift running while he got out to stack lumber. (3) He panicked when the machine jumped out of gear and started moving. (4) He tried to climb back up onto the moving forklift. (5) His foot slipped, and he fell. (6) The machine kept going, crushed him, and dragged him fifteen feet until it crashed against a concrete wall.

I'm thinking all this as I pack up cat-food man's order. Probably my professional smile has turned into a seriously unattractive frown. That wouldn't matter, except guess who's next in my line?

Alan raises his eyebrows at the cans of cat food. He's wearing this striped polo that clings nicely to his baseball muscles. His hair looks a little different, gelled or something.

"What's up?" I ask when he steps up to the register. I take my time scanning his Hershey bar and Pepsi.

"Sugar attack," he says. "Plus they say this is where all the pretty girls work."

"Nope, that's CVS. Around the corner."

"Guess I'll send that line back to the factory."

How about the line where he tells me if we're really, really just friends, or if maybe he wants to be something more? But I've got one eye on the lookout for my boss Mr. Vargas, who'll have a fit if he sees me flirting when I should be scanning. I say, "I got to get back to work."

"When do you get off?" he asks.

"Eight." I take my time handing him his change.

"Want to go to hang out at Strawberry?"

Strawberry Park is this nothing patch of land with a soccer field, busted-up walking path, and two swing sets. But it's about halfway between our houses, and we've met up there a couple of times before, usually when I'm so fed up with Cecilia I could scream or when Alan wants to do some drawing.

"OK," I say, "but we've got to stop for some food. I've got another two hours to work, and I'm already starving."

"Deal. Pick you up out front."

A few minutes later, I notice something at the end of the checkout belt.

———

"Hey, you forgot your stuff, Mr. I-Have-A-Sudden-Craving." I toss Alan the Kroger's bag with his soda and candy and climb into his truck. A nasal, twangy voice is singing on the radio.

"Since when do you like country?" I ask.

"Just keeping an open mind. What do you want to hear?"

"Doesn't matter." When you're always catching a ride with someone, it's best not to have too much of an opinion on anybody's music.

"You're stuck with the honky-tonk blues, then."

The music gets drowned out for a second by the squealing of the truck's stripped fan belts as Alan pulls out of the parking lot.

On the way from McDonald's to the park, there's this awkward silence. I want things to be good between us so much that I don't know what to say. So I press my forehead against the cool window and look out.

Empty storefronts and rangy trees pass behind the shadowy image of my face in the glass. The reflection is just a pair of floating brown eyes, a line for a nose, a hazy mouth. No birthmark. Seeing myself like that makes me feel almost pretty.

Which is dumb because that's not the face Alan sees. So I force myself to look at the side-view mirror where my whole face shows, birthmark and all. No sense in pretending.

The park is dark and mostly abandoned. We carry the food to the picnic tables by the swing sets. I try to fill up the silence with stories from work, but Alan's mood seems off. I climb up onto a table and dig into the chicken nuggets. I really like the little buckets of barbeque and sweet-n-sour; the nuggets are just an excuse for the sauce.

Alan wiggles the straw in his drink up and down, making that plastic squeaking noise. He kicks the seat of the picnic table. *Thud. Thud. Thud. Squeak. Thud. Thud. Thud.* Then his eyes drift to the soccer field, where gusts of wind are chasing leaves.

"So . . ." I want to be funny, to lighten things up. All I can think of is this stupid math joke I heard from Ms. Ford. "What did the zero say to the eight?"

"What?" Alan pitches a chicken nugget into the weeds.

"He said, 'nice belt!' Get it?" I say, but Alan's not listening. All of a sudden he jumps down from the table.

"I need a sec," he mumbles. He stomps down a grassy slope, hands jammed in his pockets.

By the time I catch up, he's already crying. I reach for his arm, but he pulls away. He kicks a pinecone, chases it, and kicks at it again. His back is to me, and his shoulders are shaking.

"Talk to me," I say from a few steps behind him.

But when he still doesn't respond, I cut in front of him so that I can see his face. "What is it?"

He blinks fast, but tiny tears still cling to his eyelashes. He tightens his jaw and finally speaks.

"Jessica's pregnant."

"What?"

"She's pregnant."

"I can't believe—I mean, I'm so sorry, Alan." My hands turn clammy, and I have to work to keep my mouth from hanging open. Jessica is Alan's little sister, the baby of a family with three boys. She's a sophomore, not even sixteen.

"She's sure?"

He scrapes his shoe back and forth over the same patch of grass until there's nothing but dirt left. "My mom sent me to pick her up from the clinic right after I stopped by to see you. She told Mom she needed to go get another one of those allergy shots for these headaches she gets. *Nada de nada*, right? Well, I pick Jess up, and she's totally nuts. At first, I couldn't understand a word she said. Finally I got the truth out of her. Pregnant, four months pregnant. I mean, shit!" He stomps on a pinecone and grinds his heel down on it. "She's just a kid, you know?"

"It's not right, it's like . . ." My stomach twists and I don't know what to say. Jessica is one of those girls who changes completely after her fifteenth birthday and everything that comes with a quinceañera. One day she was a sweet girl, the next she was a highlighted, straightened, tweezed, made-up, made-over wannabe woman dying to be noticed.

"Who's the father?" I ask.

"Carlos."

"Carlos Arreaga?"

He nods and looks ready to be sick.

I've seen Jessica hanging out with Carlos and his crew of "seniors." These are fools so far behind in their course credits that they're barely classified as juniors. They're proud of their nearly negative GPA's and reputation for skipping school for weeks on end. Carlos is maybe the worst, always weaseling his hands up some girl's skirt.

One look in those red-rimmed, pot-polluted eyes is all you need to know he's a creep.

"I asked her, you know. Why did she do it? Did she even want to be with him? She said 'no,' then 'yes,' then 'I don't know.' I had to shake her to get her to talk sense. Then she said that she wanted to do it, but only if he used protection. But he wouldn't, fed her some crap about wanting her to know the full experience. He told her she should either trust him or forget about being with him." Alan turns and looks straight at me. The moon lights up the tracks of tears down his cheeks.

"I should have kept a closer eye on her. Turns out this went on for months. After school, when Jess was supposed to be at a friend's house. She said she just never knew how to tell him no after the first time. I asked her, didn't she know she'd get pregnant? Oh hell, she cried then. Said he promised he'd be careful, that he wouldn't get her into any trouble. As if that asshole gave a shit." His voice cracks a little. "My baby sister, *sabes*?"

"I know, I know," I say. My hands are in my pockets, but I want to pull him close.

"My mom tries to understand, but Jess just keeps pushing her away. Ma raised me and Jimmy and Alex to be good guys, but somehow she didn't know what to do with Jess, how to get through to her. It's going to break her heart, I know it. When we got home, I got as far as the door with Jessica, and then I just turned around and left. I didn't want to be there. Couldn't stay home and watch that happen."

I know exactly what he means. It's like Jose and the mess he made just by faking that he knew how to use a freaking forklift. Jess, wanting to be all grown, ends up screwing everything up. And there's no pleasure in saying I told you so. None at all.

Alan closes his eyes and wipes his hands over his face. He edges a little closer to me, his voice coming out in a hoarse whisper.

"It's sick, how this happens all the time. Your sister, my sister. And all the other big bellies at school. It's that asshole Carlos that pisses me off. Just another *pinche cabrón* doing whatever the hell he wants. Can't be bothered to slap on a damn rubber; who cares if somebody's kid sister gets pregnant?"

"It's messed up," I say.

Alan takes some deep breaths, and then we start walking back to the picnic tables. I get brave and sort of wrap my arm around his back. It slows us down, but he doesn't pull away.

We sit on top of a table, and Alan starts untying and retying his shoelaces. "I didn't want to dump all this on you," he says. "I just didn't know what to do."

"Come on, Alan. You've listened to me plenty. I'm here for you."

"No, I mean, this isn't why I wanted to come here."

"Well, I'm really glad that you trust me, that you told me."

"Great news, huh?" He tries to laugh, but it comes out choked and strained.

"I mean it. I'm glad to be here for you." I rub his back, wishing I could just take the hurt from him. Because I know how it is when these things happen to somebody in your family. It might as well be happening to you, because there's no way to separate yourself. With family, you get a share in everybody's problems.

There's this long pause.

"It's so hard to know what to do," I say.

"No, it's not."

He reaches over and takes my hand in his, stroking it with his thumb. He lifts it and presses it against his mouth. His other hand wanders over to my cheek and traces the outline of my birthmark carefully, like he's painting it on me for the first time. Then he tilts my chin up toward him and kisses me with his warm, dry lips.

"Just kiss me back," he says.

January

chapter 9

"Come on, Gustavo, I really need to study for my calc test tomorrow." I jiggle the knob, but his bedroom door is locked.

"Can't do it," he calls. "I've got a job lined up in like twenty minutes. Transmission work. The guy's paying me a hundred bucks plus extra parts."

"Call and tell him you'll do it later. Please. You said you'd watch her. She's your niece, too."

"Give it up, Mari. I got stuff to do."

"God! Why is it always my job to watch her? I can't do calculus and cook dinner and babysit and . . ."

Gustavo cranks his music way up, drowning me out. I kick his door hard. "Why are you such a *pendejo*!" I shout, but I know he can't even hear me.

I give the door another kick and spin around, nearly tripping over Anita, who's standing right behind me, sucking her pinky finger and holding Paco by his neck.

Shit.

"I thought you were going to draw me a new *casita* to add to my collection," I say real soft. Less than a minute ago she was coloring at the kitchen table. Usually once she gets started she's good for at least half an hour.

I kneel down and reach for her hand, but her body is stiff, and she doesn't move. Then I smell that sharp, sour smell. I look down. Yep. Her pink sweatpants are wet from the crotch to the ankles.

"*Ay*, Anita, not again. You're a big girl now; big girls don't do that."

She starts crying. Wailing. She squirms back against the wall when I try to pick her up.

"Shhh," I whisper, "*Cálmate, cálmate*. That's my girl." It takes a while for her to relax, but finally she lets me carry her into the bathroom.

Here's the thing: Anita has been perfectly potty-trained since she was three. But yesterday Cecilia's neighbor Mrs. Salinas told me that if Anita keeps wetting herself, she won't babysit anymore. Anita's too old to piss her pants, she said, and she's too old to clean it up. Without Mrs. Salinas we're screwed, because she keeps Anita in the gap between when Mami has to go to work and when I get off from school.

"What about you? What do you need, *mi corazón*?" I whisper into Anita's hair as I clean her up. "You just get

carried all over the place, all the grown-ups so busy, huh?"
I rinse her pants and undies in the sink, wring them out,
and then toss them in the hamper.

I find a semi-clean pair of shorts and tug them onto
Anita's chubby legs. She's not crying anymore, but she
won't look at me. I sit down next to her on the bathroom
floor.

"Anita *bonita*, are you sad?"

She nods, eyes still down. The hand that's not stran-
gling Paco slips over her mouth. Seeing her wet her pants,
seeing her cry, seeing her still worried about those stupid
silver teeth, it all makes me feel angry and guilty at the
same time.

"Listen, Anita, will you make a deal with me?"

She stares at the stain on the carpet where the water
from the bathtub leaks out a little sometimes.

I tilt her chin up so she's looking at me. "You love
your *libros*, right? You know how you're always waiting for
somebody to read them to you? Well, what if I help you
learn to read them all by yourself?"

Anita takes in a shaky breath and moves her hand
away from her mouth. "Good," she whispers.

"There's just one thing," I say. "A girl who's learning
to read is way too big to wet her pants. So you're going to
have to really work on that."

"OK." Anita jabs her fingers into the carpet. "Can we
start now?"

When Gustavo walks past the kitchen table on his way out, I don't even look up from the picture book in front of us. Forget him.

I show Anita the word "cat," and together we sound it out. Then she finds the word "cap" in the book and sounds it out herself. She doesn't even cover her mouth when she smiles.

We're so busy with the alphabet and the naughty cat in the story that I almost forget about calculus. Almost. Out of the corner of my eye, I can see my math book through the mesh of my backpack. My mind drifts to Ms. Ford and the list of requirements for the UT engineering program, but I push the thought away. Calculus can wait. Anita can't.

chapter 10

Just fifteen minutes left, and my test is nearly blank.

I meant to study after work last night, but stupid Mr. Vargas made me stay late to help clean before some company inspection tomorrow, and then I slept through my alarm clock again this morning.

I bite my lip and try another problem. I write some stuff down, but I don't have a clue. Stupid calculus. Staring at the empty test makes me feel even crappier, so I raise my hand and turn it in.

Right before the bell rings, Ms. Ford slips me a note telling me to come see her during lunch.

———

At 12:30 I walk over to Ms. Ford's room. When she sees me, she puts down her sandwich and points to the two living-room chairs crammed by her desk for conferences.

I take the nearest one, brown leather with white stuffing poking out in spots. Ms. Ford sits in the one that has a floral design and blue ink stains on the arms.

"So, can you explain to me what happened today?" she asks.

"What do you mean?" I say. I can't meet her eyes, so I look down and watch her foot jiggling like crazy.

"The test."

I shrug and start tugging at one of the fluffy tufts sticking out of the chair.

"Hey! Don't pick at my chair!" She sounds genuinely pissed off.

"Sorry." I tear threads from a worn spot on my jeans instead.

Ms. Ford pulls a paper off of her desk and drops it into my lap. There's a grade circled at the top in ugly red ink: 29. I hand it back and stare at the hole in my jeans.

"This isn't like you at all. First missing homework and tutorials, now this."

"I, it's just . . ." My voice goes into hiding.

"Well?"

"It was hard," I say, hating the words as soon as they leave my mouth.

"Newsflash: this is AP calculus. But you quit after three problems!" Her foot shakes harder, rubbing up against the side of the chair. I wonder how much more friction it'd take for the chair to just burst into flames.

"I couldn't do it, that's all. I tried to get ready for the test, but it didn't work out."

"You have to be smart with your time."

"I couldn't, miss. There was no chance to study," I say.

"You've got a lot going on. Stuff at home, your boyfriend. But you can't get so caught up in everything and everybody else that you lose sight of *your* goals."

I don't say anything. So I'm supposed to tell Anita, sorry, but reading with you doesn't fit in with my goals? I pull another thread from the hole in my pants.

I can feel Ms. Ford staring at me. It gives me that shitty feeling you get when somebody thinks they know everything about you, but you know they've got it all wrong. She's thinking my life could be simple if I would just follow some stupid goal-planning worksheet and come to tutorials. She's thinking, *These Mexican girls, why won't they take their futures seriously?* She's thinking, *This Marisa, if she were more like me, she'd go far.*

"You can't give up on yourself," she says.

"I'm working really hard, but . . ."

"I wish it were easier, but you've just got to make hard decisions. Education is your ticket."

Like I don't know that! It's like she's reading right off one of those stupid motivational posters from middle school. I can feel the heat in my cheeks, and I want to tell her to back the fuck off. Those are the very words fighting to get off my tongue. Because she doesn't know my life. She doesn't know me.

I fight to keep the anger in and cook up my most serious sincere-student look. "I'll try harder," I say. I force my eyes to meet hers.

"Don't just try, do it. There's a big difference." Her lips are set in a tight line that makes me think of a minus sign. All of a sudden the minus sign goes blurry, and my eyes are wet.

"Look." The white smudge that is Ms. Ford's face moves closer to me. "You can retake the test. You're a good worker; you're just stretching yourself too thin. I know how it is."

But she doesn't. She doesn't.

"Just come in tomorrow after school and try the test again."

"I can't, miss." I blink until the tears clear.

She looks surprised. "Monday, then."

"I still can't, OK? I just can't."

"Marisa, you've got to . . ."

"Trust me, I want to. The problem is that it's not just me that I have to worry about. I have responsibilities to other people, promises I can't break."

"I'm on your side, remember?" Ms. Ford says. There's nothing mean in her voice now; she just sounds disappointed. "But you have to do your part. And it's going to get easier once you're in college. At UT . . ."

"I don't care about UT! You want me to be this perfect success story, the college girl from the *barrio*." My voice rises, and I don't realize until I say this next thing just how

64

much it's bothering me. "UT didn't send me nothing, get it? They probably don't want me, so do me a favor and forget about it!"

"Marisa!"

I grab my bag and head for the door before she can say anything else.

———

Ms. Ford's words eat at me all day long. My mood is so foul that all I can think to do is scribble black lines in the margin of my physics notebook until my pen tears through the paper. I try awarding myself some imaginary blue ribbons for being such a super aunt, but that doesn't make me feel any better.

Somebody has gotten Mr. Gordon off the topic of thermodynamics by bringing up motorcycles, which he'll gladly talk about until he forgets to assign the homework. Usually I'd rather learn physics, but today I don't care. I scrawl "UT" over and over just so I can X it out. Ms. Ford never should have even mentioned UT to me in August. Just one more thing to want and not get. She had me all excited about solving real-world problems, designing bridges, all kinds of bullshit. Maybe Alan will draw me a picture of Ms. Ford so I can put her face on Gustavo's dartboard and use her for a target.

The P.A. system clicks on, and the principal starts talking about an all-day practice standardized test scheduled for Monday. We start groaning, because what this means is being stuck in homeroom all day, filling in bubbles on a stupid Scantron sheet. But then good old Mr. Dominguez crackles back over the intercom and says, "The seniors are exempt from the test and will now receive additional instructions for their activities on Monday."

Mr. Gordon reads from a printout, and the scoop on Monday is way better than just getting out of the test. Seniors who are passing all of their required courses get the entire day off. All we have to do is come to the school office on Monday morning to sign the attendance roster. That way, as far as the state is concerned, we came to school. Because in Texas, attendance equals money. Whatever, as long as we don't have to spend the day in school or sitting on the bleachers in the gym waiting for everybody else to finish the exam. By the time Mr. Gordon gets to the end of his announcement, nobody is listening. "Free day" is all that matters. The class buzzes with plans for the unofficial holiday, and cell phones pop up under desks. I text "WOOHOO!" to Brenda and Alan. After today, I deserve a break.

chapter 11

On Monday I leave for school at my usual time because I don't want my parents to know about the senior holiday. There are at least three things I should be doing with my time off: (1) working extra hours, (2) watching Anita so that Mami can go to Mass like she likes to, (3) busting my butt studying calculus.

But I'm too mad at Ms. Ford to even look at my math book, and I have this feeling that's crowding out my thoughts of Mami and work. It's so strong that if I was in a cartoon, there'd probably be rays of light coming out of my chest.

At school I sign the roster and stop for a second to talk to Brenda. She says Alan has already come and gone. I ignore her exaggerated winks and start walking.

When I turn onto Alan's street, I see that only his truck is in the driveway. I'm so relieved I almost laugh out loud. I mean, I want to surprise him, but I would have choked on my *buenos días* if his mom or dad had answered the door.

I walk fast, passing homes just like the ones in my neighborhood, flat-roofed houses with patchy grass in the front and carports overflowing with junk. Vicente Fernandez's voice drifts out of a window along with the smell of burnt *chorizo*.

I knock twice before Alan answers. He opens the door and pulls down his earphones. "Hey, you," he says. "I thought you were working."

"Nope," I say really softly. I'm afraid he doesn't want to see me, but I try to sound cheerful. "Here I am!"

He kisses my cheek and invites me inside, and I'm OK again. We've been an "us" for over a month, but when he touches me I still feel all shivery and warm at the same time.

"You want a Coke?" He's already tossing ice cubes into a glass.

"Sure. Jimmy didn't put you to work at El Ranchero?" El Ranchero is this big Mexican restaurant that's popular with Mexican families and white people, too. It's always busy, and Alan's brother Jimmy always has work for him there.

"Nah, I told him I might not feel like playing ball for him anymore if he didn't give me the day off."

"That's such a lie," I say. Alan complains all the time about having his brother for a boss and a baseball coach, but really he loves it. Jimmy is cool, even though he picks on him.

"True," he says. "But I got to keep Jimmy in line. I can't let him get too used to bossing me around. Next thing I know he'll be telling me how to tuck in my uniform and comb my hair, stuff that's way too personal. Coming from him, I mean."

"So I can tell you how to tuck your shirt in?"

"Hell, you can do it for me *si quieres*." He grins.

"I hope you don't have any secrets back here." I cross the kitchen to the door to his room. I've been in there once before, the only other time nobody else was home when I came over.

It's an old porch that Alan, Jimmy, and his dad closed in a few years back. It's cramped, and the floor sort of slants to one side, but Alan doesn't care. He likes the extra windows and the door to the backyard because he can sneak out at night to draw when he can't sleep. I know because every once in a while I get a text message at two or three in the morning with a photo of what he's drawing. I like to imagine him out there in the silent yard, his face half glowing with moonlight, half darkened by shadows.

Alan touches my shoulder with the cold glass of Coke, and I jump.

"Welcome back to Palace Peralta," he says, kicking open the door.

"Yeah right." I sweep two dirty socks and a T-shirt off of his desk chair and then take my glass of Coke with both hands. The damp coolness of it feels good against my clammy skin.

"What're you working on?" I ask. His sketchbook is propped up against a heap of blankets on his bed.

"Nothing important."

I shoot him an uh-uh look. "Don't even say that. Your drawings are so good. Let me see?"

Alan flips the book open to an ink drawing and hands it over.

There's a girl in the middle, and even though her face is clenched in pain, I recognize Alan's little sister. Jessica's body is stretched out, and her legs are super-long and twisting like rubber down toward the left corner of the page. Her pregnant belly swells huge in the center, and her arms are lifted in a way that reminds me of Anita when she wants to be picked up. There's a giant faucet, and under it, a huge bathtub drain. Then I get it.

She's being sucked down the drain. Behind her, smaller, there are other girls, a lot of them. They have different faces, but the pregnant belly is the same, and they're all twisting down toward the drain. Around the edges of the page, the words SAME OLD STORY repeat over and over. I can't look away from it.

"God," I whisper.

"Yeah, I know it's weird, just scribbling," he says. He starts to close the sketchbook.

"No." I stop his hand. "Not weird at all. It gets to me. You aren't scribbling, you're ..." My voice quits on me, but suddenly I get brave and scramble from the chair over onto the bed.

"It's the best thing you've ever shown me. It's real, like, it means something. It makes me want to look and keep looking." With my pinky finger, I trace the shape of the girl in the center. She's Jessica, but at the same time she's Cecilia and every pregnant girl I've ever known.

"Sometimes," he says, "I just have to draw. If I don't, it's like the feelings start to choke me."

The sun filtering through his windows lights up all the pieces of dust in the air so that they look like gold acrobats. Sophomore year, our biology teacher told us that most of the dust in a house is actually pieces of us, skin cells and stuff. Maybe it's sick, but I take a deep breath in and imagine golden Alan-acrobats dancing through the darkness inside me.

We're both sitting cross-legged, like in kindergarten sharing circle, and I move closer to him until our knees are lined up. I tell myself to be brave. I put a finger over his lips. I link my eyes with his, and the look that goes between us is so strong that I swear I can feel his eyelashes brush against my cheek. When I set my right hand on his left knee, he puts his right hand on my left knee. Then he waits.

I just watch him for a minute, loving how he's looking at me the same way he looks at a drawing, like he's seeing things nobody else can see. I love how his brown eyes smile before his lips do, and there's this easy strength to his body that makes me crazy. I'm dying to kiss the chicken pox scar just below his mouth.

My whole body is tingling from wanting him so bad. I lean closer. So does he. I smile. So does he. I slide my hand up from the knee, inching closer to his body. I close my eyes. His fingertips move slowly up my thigh, and I think I feel them tremble, like they're still learning their way, too.

We're kissing and moving against each other, and I feel like something is changing in me, like all that light I felt earlier just thinking about Alan has dropped about a foot and a half and is now making me hot in X-rated places. I'm thinking that this is going way too fast, that this is not what I meant for us to do, not exactly. And I'm wondering what Alan's thinking when, all of a sudden, the hand that he was sliding down my back slips under my leg. When he starts tickling me behind my knee, I laugh and almost bite his tongue before I pull back.

He leans against the wall and pulls me close until I'm basically in his lap. His arms wrap around my stomach, and he rests his chin on the top of my head. I can feel his breath on my scalp. We sit there and watch two squirrels play in the backyard.

A lot of things pop into my head. Like how glad I am that we didn't have to have some awkward talk, that we just stopped before we got too crazy. Like maybe we both knew enough from our sisters' lives to be over the "caught in the moment" thing. Like how soft the inside of his elbow is and how amazing it is to feel his thumb rubbing mine.

But these are not the kinds of things you can casually mention, so I lean my head back against his chest and say, "How about you tell me a story."

"A story?" He drums his fingers on my stomach. "Hmmm . . . OK, I've got one. There once was an old man from Peru who dreamed he was eating a shoe."

"That's the whole story?"

"No. Now if you'll let me finish, please." He says it like he's annoyed, but I can feel him smiling into my hair. "There once was an old man from Peru who dreamed he was eating his shoe. He woke up that night in a terrible fright and found out it was perfectly true!"

"Very funny," I say. One of the squirrels jumps up onto the windowsill and flashes signals with his tail. "That squirrel just called you lame. He said you should tell a real story. About us."

"Well, if the squirrel said so . . ." He starts to reach behind my knee, but in a flash I have my fingers poised to tickle under his arms, so he doesn't even try it.

"Good defense," he says.

"Don't try to change the subject. We're waiting."

"OK, this time for real." Alan cracks his knuckles like he does before he puts on his baseball glove.

"Once upon a time, there was a beautiful lady and a kindhearted, shaggy-haired beast."

"No," I interrupt, "it should be a beautiful lady and a kindhearted, shaggy-haired *gentleman*."

"Fine," he says, "now be quiet and listen." His voice deepens a little as he settles into storytelling mode. "This gentleman loved the lady, right, but he was really poor, more of a servant boy. Every day he wanted to make her laugh. He saved up his best lines for the few moments when he saw her. Sometimes it was when he carried firewood into the room where she had her daily lessons. Other times, she came out to the stable to ride her golden horse."

His voice makes me feel happy and safe, and I let myself slip with him into a make-believe world.

"The servant boy lived for any chance to see the lady. At first he was shy, but he got braver and talked to her more. So even though he didn't have any money, when she laughed it made him feel rich.

"After a while, the servant boy figured out that the lady liked him too. Sometimes she called for a fire, and after he brought the wood in and arranged it, she changed her mind just so that she had an excuse to call him back later. In the stable, she asked for his help to climb up onto her horse even though she'd done it on her own for years. The way they looked at each other said what their jokes couldn't.

"One day the lady snuck out to the boy's cottage even though that was so taboo that he could have gotten killed. The lady begged the servant boy for a story that would make her laugh. So they walked out to a grassy hill where there was a nice summer breeze.

"The boy told her stories about forest animals, fairies, and stupid peasants. And then he started telling the lady about some lovers from a distant country and a distant time, hundreds of years beyond them. But the lady started to cry. She didn't like how the lovers' lives made them suffer.

"The boy kissed her and said, 'My lady, everything has another side. Their troubles draw them together.'

"Now the lady was really bawling, because she knew that she and the servant boy could never be so lucky. He got scared and tried to dry her tears with handfuls of wildflowers.

"But she kept crying until the tears flooded the ground around them, creating a river that swept them down the hill. They slid and slid until they had traveled out of the kingdom, and then suddenly they slipped right into the future. And that's where they woke up, damp with the lady's tears, clinging to each other in a small bedroom very much like this one."

When he finishes, there's a long stretch of quiet between us. A good kind of quiet. Safe and warm, the sweetness of his words tucked around me. If I didn't have to go to work, I think I could stay here forever.

"Alan Peralta," I say, "you are full of surprises."

chapter 12

A week later, Alan waits in his truck while I walk up the cracked sidewalk to Mrs. Salinas's apartment to get Anita. It's been forever since she's been to the park, and today's clear and warm, more like March than January. The high-school baseball season starts in two weeks, and I think Alan must be skipping practice to take us, but he swears Jimmy cancelled it.

"Door's open, *mija*," Mrs. Salinas shouts when I knock.

It's the usual scene. Mrs. Salinas is propped up on the sofa, her big stomach resting on her legs like a lump of dough somebody forgot to make into tortillas. Univision blasts from the TV.

There's a patter of footsteps in the back bedroom, and Anita runs out with her shoes already on and her toy bag slung across her back.

"Everything OK today?" I ask Mrs. Salinas.

"No more of *that* problem, *gracias a Dios*." She doesn't take her eyes off the TV, not even when Anita says good-bye.

"See you tomorrow, then." I reach for Anita's hand and smile at her. Because if I didn't keep my face busy I'd probably be sticking my tongue out at Mrs. Salinas.

———

I kick off one shoe, then the other, and slide my feet down into the playground pebbles. Anita's so happy on her swing that she's forgotten not to smile, and her silver teeth flash in the sun. Everybody is out today, kids playing soccer on the balding field, older ladies walking their loops on the little concrete trail that rings the park, people just off from work bringing their dogs to the park to crap in the weeds.

I wave at Anita, then go back to bitching about Ms. Ford's class. I can't just skip it, but I wait until the last possible moment to go into her room so she can't corner me and stuff me full of another lecture.

Alan plays with a handful of stones. "So you're having a rough time. You like Ms. Ford; that just makes it worse."

"She expects too much. I used to like that, but now it's making me feel like crap, like I'll never meet her standards. Maybe I should just let it go."

"Exactly, don't let it eat at you. Just go see her and smooth things over."

"No, I mean let the class go."

Alan drops his handful of rocks. "You're joking." He stares at me like I just said it's stupid to be Mexican or something.

"It's just an elective. I don't need it to graduate."

"Marisa, you love that class."

"*Used* to love it. Not no more, not with Ms. Ford judging me."

"You don't know that. She just wants to help you. You told her what's going on with Cecilia and everything?"

"She knows my family is a mess, but not the details. It's . . ."

"Embarrassing."

"Yeah."

"I know," he says. "I don't want to be the guy whose kid sister got knocked up any more than you want to be the kid sister of the girl who got knocked up, married the jerk, and now has to work at a gas station to support him."

"Ouch," I say. I tip my head back and stare up at the sky. Mami used to say that my guardian angel was hiding in the clouds and watching over me. That was fine most of the time, but then I would get scared on days like this when there weren't any clouds.

But now I know nobody gets a special angel. The sky sees everybody's problems and doesn't care about any of them.

"Do you ever just think, 'This is my life, and it sucks?' Like when your mom and dad are arguing about Jessica, or she's saying she wants to move in with Carlos? Crap like that?"

"Sure." He scoops up more rocks and starts sorting them by shades of gray. "But it's not my life that sucks. It's my sister's life. Or maybe my parents' life. Me, I'm not trapped."

"See, I can't break myself away like that. Jose is Cecilia's problem, but when it comes to Anita, I can't just say she's somebody else's problem, you know?"

Alan tosses the rocks back and dusts off his hands. "You don't have to rescue everybody. Nobody can do that. Don't forget about your stuff, your goals and shit."

I roll my eyes. "Now you sound like Ms. Ford. It's like you're saying, 'Don't worry about your niece, just do math.' That's not something I can do. Anita deserves to be taken care of right."

I look over to check on her. She's still pumping away on the swing. I wouldn't mind joining her.

Alan traps my leg with his big bare feet, then releases it. "You're making things too black and white. I mean, you can help your family without quitting on your dreams."

"I have dreams?" I snort in this unattractive piggy way I immediately wish I could take back.

"I'm not joking, Mari. We can stick together; it can be different for us."

He sounds serious in a way that turns on those bright lights in my heart and at the same time makes me feel like I'm about to pee my pants. My hands get damp, and I don't know what to say.

Just then the kids in the swings by Anita jump down and run off.

"Come on," I shout. "This is our chance!"

I scoop up my shoes and grab Alan's hand. Together we stumble barefoot and laughing toward the swing set.

"Anita *bonita*!" I call.

"Underdog, Alan! Underdog!" Anita squeals.

Alan grabs onto the rubber seat of her swing and then runs under her, pushing her high into the air. He gives me an underdog, too, and the rush of air around me and the blue of the sky and the sound of Anita laughing all make it seem like I don't need a guardian angel anyway.

February

chapter 13

The first varsity baseball game of the season lands on Valentine's Day. I tell Alan ahead of time that I have to work, which is true, but I don't tell him that I've got things worked out to leave a little early so that I can make the last part of the game. Brenda drops me off at the field before she goes off with Greg for the night, but she doesn't let me out of the car until I change out of my Kroger uniform and into a pink-and-gray sweater she brought for me.

I guess Brenda's not the only one whose priority is her hot date, because attendance at the game is seriously weak. It's easy for me to spot Alan's family right on the front row of bleachers. It doesn't hurt that his dad is standing with his arms crossed, shaking his head. "Let's go, Lobos," he shouts. "This is your last shot!"

Alan's mom tugs him back down onto the seat, and Jessica rolls her eyes and scoots a little farther away from them both like she wishes she could be anywhere except at a baseball game with her parents.

I glance up at the scoreboard. The score is five to three, and we're losing. But it's only the seventh inning, so I figure we've got time. I slide onto the bleachers between Jessica and her mom.

"Marisa, hi," Alan's mom says. "I didn't know you were coming." She gives me a little squeeze after I kiss her cheek. Alan's dad takes my hand and greets me, but his eyes are glued to the field. Our first batter is just coming up to the plate.

"How's it going, Jess?" I ask.

She shrugs and plays with the little sapphire-studded ring on her pinky finger.

"You look really cute; I love that shirt," I tell Jess a minute later, which is all the time it takes for our first two batters to strike out. Jess is wearing a baby-doll top that's loose and full, so if you didn't know she was pregnant, you wouldn't be able to tell yet.

"Thanks," she says. "It's weird, you know, trying to figure out what to wear now that I'm . . . fat."

I see Alan's mom flinch a little, but she doesn't say anything to Jess. "If this kid doesn't strike out, Alan'll be up next, *mija*," she tells me, nodding at the on-deck circle. Alan's practicing his swing, and I try to beam him hard-core kick-ass thoughts so that he can knock the ball out of the park when he goes up to bat.

But he doesn't get the chance because four pitches later, the last batter hits a high ball out to right field, and the right fielder catches it.

"Dang it all," Alan's dad says. Both teams start streaming out of their dugouts, and at first I think they're just switching sides, but then they line up to shake hands.

"Mr. Peralta? Why'd they quit early?" I ask. I point to the scoreboard. "I thought there'd be two more innings."

He shakes his head. "I wish. Just seven innings in high school baseball."

Damn. I didn't think about that. So much for my sports knowledge—or for getting to see Alan play.

"Well, how'd Alan do?" I ask.

"We didn't win," his dad says. He wipes a hand on the spirit T-shirt that Alan designed and rolls up the last of his sunflower seeds in their plastic bag. "He did fine, though, no errors. Jimmy'll be giving them all what for now, but you can cheer Alan up afterward." He gives me a wink.

I blush and am trying to figure out what I can say to that when Alan walks over to us and throws his bag down on the bleachers. "So here's my fan club."

"Good game, son," his dad says, slapping him on the back. "Just got to get the batting worked out."

His mom gives him a little sideways hug. "You've got your truck? We'll see you at the house later?"

He nods and wipes off his forehead. His hair is sticking up in these crazy little peaks around the edges, and I can see a faint line of salt down one cheek where his sweat dried. "Thanks for coming, you guys. Sorry it wasn't a better show."

Alan plops down and starts pulling off his cleats. "You still want to be my girl? Even though I'm a loser?"

"Shut up," I say. I kiss him right on his sweaty forehead, and the heat of him makes me feel a little crazy. "Anyway, I barely got here, so I didn't witness you doing any losing. Sorry."

"Don't be. Hey, I've got something for you."

"No way, it's my turn to give something to you." I sit down next to him and unzip my backpack. Alan already sent me four carnations and bought me one of the teddy bears Brenda's nursing club was selling for their latest fund-raiser. All I gave him was a card, plus a Valentine from Anita that said, "ALN beall mInE!" so I got a heart-shaped pack of X and O donuts from Krispy Kreme to sort of balance things out. XOXO— hugs and kisses. Pretty cheesy, I know, but he is crazy over Krispy Kreme. I pull them out of my bag and hand them to him.

"Sweet, this is just what I need!" The three O's disappear, and all that's left in the box is XXX. "Hey, that's a little more serious than hugs and kisses, *verdad*?" He grins and offers me one of his donuts. "OK, can I give you my thing now?"

He doesn't wait for me to answer, and he pulls out a big red envelope. Inside is a giant card with pink and red butterflies inked on a white background. Each one has these crazy intricate designs inside its wings. Like everything Alan draws, it's beautiful. Inside there's a simple message in block letters: "Marisa, be my *mariposa*."

"I love it," I say, and I do. "Every inch of it's beautiful."

"Like you," he says.

"Right, I think the sugar's going to your head. Or else seeing that triple X just pushed you over the edge." We kiss, though—a long, sweet-and-salty kiss that has my thoughts going all X-rated.

"I got to take you home, huh?" he says soft into my ear.

"Yeah, sorry. Thirty more minutes and I turn into a pumpkin."

"I'll take you out on Saturday for Valentine's, OK? If you can?"

When Saturday rolls around, not even a double shift at Kroger can touch my good mood. I walk home from the bus stop, seriously starving and worn out from the constant rush at the store, but the sun's out, and for once the air is cool and crisp. Half an hour of rain this morning washed all of the pollution out of the air, I guess, because it seems like you can see for miles. All the way down the block, at least. And best of all, I'm in the clear to have a night out with Alan. Ceci's off today for once, so she's got Anita. And Mami was already making *pozole* this morning, which means I don't have to cook.

The first thing I see when I turn onto our street is the butt crack of some old guy in a wife-beater. He's bent down scrubbing the rims on his Ford, which is why I get the unwelcome view. The second thing I see is Alan's truck, parked in our driveway.

This is weird. We don't have plans until later, like hours from now. As far as I know, he's supposed to be working for his brother at the restaurant. I'm thinking, *shit, not another crisis, please.* I dig my phone out of my bag and check for messages. Nothing. He would have called me if something was up. And it's really not like Alan to be hanging out at my house when I'm not there, no matter how great my mom thinks he is.

I feel a twist in my stomach as I walk up into the carport. I pause just outside the back door and hear Alan and Mami speaking in Spanish.

"... needs a chance to be a parent," Alan is saying.

"Of course, *mijo*, our families will come together through this. *Así debe ser*, everyone united."

"*Sí, señora*. I don't think you'll be disappointed."

"Let me call your mother to see how we can arrange everything," Mami says back, her voice sunny and excited.

I freeze with my hand on the doorknob. Our mothers hardly know each other. What could they possibly need to arrange? I seriously don't like things going on behind my back. I narrow my eyes and push open the door.

"*¿Qué pasó?*" I ask, locking the door behind me.

Alan and Mami are sitting across from each other at the kitchen table, a plate of day-old *pan dulce* between them. They both just stare at me. Alan looks guilty and proud of himself at the same time. I can't read my mom's face. Right off she makes some excuse and hurries off to the back of the house.

"So," I say, "making plans with my mom or what?" Even though I try to keep my voice light, I'm pretty sure my words come out sounding like an accusation.

"We saved you the pineapple empanada," he says.

"Thanks," I say. "I'm not really hungry." A total lie, but I'm not ready to take what seems way too much like a peace offering. I attack the pile of dishes in the sink.

Alan comes over to the counter to help me dry, and after a few torturous moments, he starts to explain. By the time he goes through his whole idea very carefully, I've cooled off a little. Maybe I overreacted.

I lean over and give him a peck on the cheek. "That's great, Alan; that's really sweet. It's just . . ."

"Just what?" He toys with the dish towel, snapping it a little between his hands. A little shower of water droplets lands on my arm, and I wipe them off on my shirt.

I rinse the soapsuds from the last dish and hand it to him. "I just wish you would've talked to me first. Sometimes you don't get the whole picture."

"I wanted to surprise you with something that would help you. I had this crazy idea that you'd be excited." Alan dries the dish and sets it on the counter. "It's like you only go for a plan if you came up with it. You ask for help, but then you don't really want it."

"Anita gets *watched* all day long. She needs real attention and care. She needs to be with someone who will talk to her, read to her, play with her." I pull the plug, and murky dishwater swirls down the drain.

"Jessica can do all that."

"So can Ceci, but she doesn't," I shoot back.

He sits down at the table. "You've already made up your mind, I guess. But don't come complaining to me about how you don't have time to study."

"I just want the best for Anita. Nobody else is looking out for her right now. If I don't . . ."

"Listen to yourself, Marisa," he interrupts. "You're not the only one in the world who can take care of her. Jess really does need the practice. In a couple of months, she's going to be a mom for real. She can learn how to work with a kid, and you can catch up in Ms. Ford's class. Win-win. What's the problem?"

"Fine," I say, forcing a smile.

He stares at me. "That's it?"

"Thank you," I add too late. "It's a good idea."

"Yeah, I can tell you really think so," he says, crossing his arms. "Look, I got to go meet Jimmy at the restaurant to set up for some big group coming in. You still want me to pick you up later?"

I bite my lip, thinking of how fast I've managed to put a shit cloud over our night out. "*Claro*," I say, pulling his hand free and holding it tight between mine. "I can't wait." I kiss him fast, in case Mami comes around the corner, and I can see that, even though he isn't smiling, he wants to.

chapter 14

I tap my pencil against my calculus book and watch Jessica and Anita through the open doorway to the living room. They're snuggled together on the floor, backs against the couch. They make a really cute pair, Anita with her tongue hiding her silver teeth, Jessica with a sweatshirt hiding her pregnant belly. Jess is using her cell phone to make little texts for Anita to read, things like, "That rat is fat!" Anita loves the attention.

Jessica thought of that idea on her own when Anita started playing with her phone. Pretty impressive, especially since it's only the second week Jess has been helping. Before, I thought I would need to teach her how to do everything and that Anita would be mad that I wasn't spending time with her. But that's not it at all. In fact,

Anita hasn't even looked my way all afternoon, that's how busy she is having fun with Alan's sister.

I'm in the middle of a calculus problem when someone bangs on the front door. Nobody who knows us would ever use that door, so my heart races a little as I run over and look through the peephole.

Staring back at me is a giant green eye.

I swing the door open. "Seriously, Brenda!"

She's doubled over laughing. Behind her, Greg grins at me. Alan's with them, too. He shrugs like he wants to say, "This was not my idea."

"Oh my god, Marisa, I swear I could hear your heart beating through the door."

"No, *mensa*, that was you beating *on* the door."

Brenda leans past me into the living room. "Hi Anita, hi Jess!" she calls and darts inside the house. I can hear her whispering to Jessica.

"You're under arrest, ma'am," Greg says to me.

I take a good look at Greg, who's wearing a bomber jacket and black slacks. He has on shiny black boots, too. I guess he's going for the rookie police officer look. He might have passed for one—in a dark alley, to a blind person.

"Don't make us take you by force. Step away from the door."

Brenda comes back over and gives me a little push forward. "Better do what the officer says. Get into the patrol car."

I shoot her a look. "I don't see no patrol car. You can't mean that old thing." I point at Brenda's Honda.

"Undercover operation," Brenda says, sticking out her tongue.

"Alan, help me talk sense to these fools," I plead.

"I think you'd better go along with it," he says and shoves his hands into his pockets.

"Listen, you guys. I don't have time to play cops and robbers. Come back and harass me after Cecilia picks up Anita, after I get off work, and after all my homework is done."

"You leave us with no choice." Greg whips out a pair of handcuffs and slaps one onto my left wrist and the other onto Alan's right.

"There's no stopping these two. Trust me, I already tried. You might as well try to enjoy yourself," Alan says.

Brenda locks the front door with my keys. "*Vámonos!*"

"Hold up," I say. "In half an hour I really do have to go to work. And Jessica shouldn't be taking care of Anita all by herself."

"Anita hasn't even noticed you're gone. She's totally cool. Little Mama Jess is doing a badass job. Now stop worrying." Brenda steers me and Alan toward the car, and Greg opens the back door. I guess he pays attention when he watches *Cops*, because he pushes our heads down when we get in.

Once we're all strapped in, Brenda gives me an evil grin. "You wouldn't give yourself a break, so we had to take one for you. Too much studying isn't good for you."

"Remember Kroger? I'd still like to be employed there tomorrow."

"I took care of that, too."

"What did you do?" This is not good.

"Mr. Vargas?" Brenda does her make-fun-of-Marisa voice. "Hi, it's me, Marisa? I think I'm coming down with something, cough, cough, I feel pretty bad, cough, and I don't think I can make it today."

"You didn't!"

"Hell, yeah, I did. He ate it up," Brenda says. She starts singing along with the radio.

"Is that a chicken dying or you singing?" I say, poking her through the seat.

———

Ten minutes later we're driving down Texas Avenue. I haven't been downtown since my sophomore art class came for a field trip to the Museum of Fine Arts. The sun is setting, and the mirrored sides of the skyscrapers reflect pink and orange clouds.

We stop at a red light by a restaurant, and I watch men and women in suits and nice clothes lean close to each other over their fancy dinners. Soft music drifts out to the street. Maybe downtown Houston isn't Hollywood, but compared to our neighborhood, it might as well be. I start to get dizzy when I imagine what it'd be like to work in one of the big buildings. I bet those people never think about ugly south Houston when they're riding down in the glass elevator for their dinner dates.

Probably all they've got to worry over is whose turn it is to pick the restaurant.

When the light turns green, Brenda rounds the corner and pulls into a drive with a sign that says "Angelika Parking."

It turns out that the Angelika is a fancy movie theater Greg used to go to all the time when he lived with his dad. It's student night, so the tickets are cheap, and we even get free popcorn and Coke.

While we wait in line, Alan nudges Greg with his elbow. "Think the cuffs could come off?"

"Guess she can't run away now. I've just got to find the keys." He pats down his pockets and searches around in the zippered pouch of his jacket. "Uh oh," he frowns.

Alan starts to look nervous. "Come on, man."

"Shit, I'm really sorry." Greg winces. "It must be back at my mom's place."

Alan just stares at him. He looks like a little boy who can't decide between crying or punching somebody.

"Hey, no worries, no worries." Greg opens his hand and shows us the key.

Alan breathes again, and as soon as the handcuffs are off, he excuses himself.

Greg cracks up. "He thought he was going to have to take you to the pisser with him!"

When we walk out onto the street two hours later, we're laughing and repeating the best lines. Brenda's even singing bits of the soundtrack.

"I think I'm starting to agree with Marisa about this 'singing' business," Greg says.

Brenda chases him all the way to the car and whacks him on the butt with her purse.

Back on the freeway, I roll down my window and stick my arms way out to feel the air rush past.

Alan coughs. "This is Houston, not Wyoming, babe. That ain't fresh air you're letting in."

I roll up the window. "Killjoy," I say. "For that, you have to get me ice cream."

At Baskin Robbins, Greg launches into a joke marathon, and for once I actually laugh at his bit about superheroes and sex on the beach. Maybe the chocolate sundae is affecting my brain. Or maybe this is what being seventeen is supposed to feel like.

I break in with one of Ms. Ford's jokes. "Why does everyone like to be around a mushroom?"

"God, this is going to be a groaner. I can already tell," Brenda says.

"Cause he's such a *fun-gi*!" I slap my knee. "Get it? FUN-GI . . . FUN GUY!"

Brenda and Greg groan, but Alan laughs. I pull his face close and kiss him.

"You think we should get you home?" he whispers.

"I don't know, maybe." I pull my phone out of my pocket to check the time. I stop smiling. I forgot to turn the ringer back on when we left the theater, and now I'm staring at seven missed calls and a voice-mail message. All but one of the calls is from home.

The other one's from Ceci, who left a message an hour ago. "Look, I told Ma that Brenda was taking you somewhere, but you'd better call her soon. Papi wants to know where the hell you are. I guess he's pretty pissed."

"Everything OK?" Greg asks when I set the phone down.

"We'll see when I get home," I say. I force another bite of my ice cream, then push the cup away.

When we pull into my driveway ten minutes later, I lean forward to hug Brenda and Greg. "You guys rock. This was the best arrest ever."

Alan opens the door and gets out with me. He rubs his thumb against my cheek. "I can come in if you want, you know, to help explain."

"Probably everything will be fine."

"You sure?"

"Yeah. I'll text you later."

"OK, babe. See you in the morning." He tries to sound casual, but I know he's worried.

Brenda pulls the car out of the driveway, and I wave until it disappears around the corner.

———

The front of the house is dark, but buttery squares of light fall through the kitchen window and onto the driveway. It's cracked in a million places, but the landlord doesn't care enough to fix it. Papi keeps trying to fill in the cracks with this black gunk. Looks like a giant spider's web.

Before I slide my key into the back door lock, I peek at my cell phone. 11:15.

Mami and Papi are sitting at the table.

My mom looks relieved. "*Mija*, you had us worried . . ." Her words trail off as Papi's face goes dark.

"*¿Dónde estabas?*" he asks softly. But not gently. The muscles in his jaw tremble and tighten. A vein stands out on his forehead.

I try to organize my thoughts into words, but nothing comes out.

He stands up. "Do I got to speak English for you to get it? Where. Were. You."

"Papi, I . . ."

"Don't 'Papi' me. You left my granddaughter with a stranger so you could run off with your friends?" he says, switching his attack back to Spanish.

"It was a surprise, they surprised me, I didn't know about it until Brenda said—"

"I don't care what Brenda said. You listen good, *hija*. I have plenty *desgracia* with your sister. No more. I don't need no more."

"*Sí*, Papi." Suddenly I feel weak all over, like I can barely stand. I close my eyes, wishing I was back at the movies, wishing I could pretend for just a little longer that this is not my life.

"Look at me when I speak to you," my dad says.

I lift my eyes.

"You go to school. You watch Anita. You cook. You go to the store and do your hours. We will make this family work. And you will help. No more passing off our family's business onto other people. *No más.*"

"I've always helped, Papi," I whisper, trying to keep my voice steady.

Mami starts to say something, but Papi shuts her down with a look. He grabs the edge of my shirt sleeve and then lets it go like it's too dirty to touch. "You have these big ideas that you're too good now. Got it in school, maybe, or from that Brenda. You think you can run around like a *sinvergüenza* without a thought for your family." The corners of his mouth tip down, and his nose wrinkles in disgust. He turns away from me so fast that he knocks over one of the chairs.

"No more," he says, looking back for a second. "No more." He ignores the fallen chair and disappears into the dark hallway. The bedroom door clicks shut.

I stare after him, vaguely feeling Mami's hand on my shoulder. The fingers of her other hand wipe away tears that I didn't even know were there.

chapter 15

"It's all my fault," Brenda says, sliding her lunch tray back and forth between her hands. "Look where my great idea got you."

"I was the one who kept us out for ice cream," I say.

"Jesus," Greg says, "you went to a movie, for crap's sake. You didn't go to a bar!"

"I might as well have, the way my dad sees things," I pick at the crust of my sandwich.

"Mexican papis are not like white daddies," Brenda explains to Greg. "Mexican dads don't want their daughters 'running around.' Sometimes they think they're still living in Mexico in little *ranchos* where the women cook beans and make tortillas all day."

"You're Mexican, but your dad isn't like that," Greg says.

"Half Mexican," she corrects. "And lucky you. It's because my mommy is an ass-whooping Cubana who doesn't take orders from nobody."

They start kissing, and I let the roar of the cafeteria erase everything in my mind. When I see Alan across the sea of tables, I take off.

———

We sit back-to-back under an oak tree behind the school. There's not much around but weeds, trash, and damp grass, but at least it's quiet. I close my eyes, and Alan leans his head on my shoulder.

"I should have told Brenda no, not to put you in that position," he says.

"I'm not a bad daughter," I say.

"You do everything you can. Sometimes too much." Alan laces his fingers through mine.

"I wish I could ignore the things he said. I shouldn't even care. But it's like I can never shake loose of him."

"He's your dad, Marisa."

"Unfortunately. My mom is always reminding me about his bad childhood, how his stepmother barely fed him or his brothers, how he never had shoes."

"That could really mess a person up."

"But shouldn't he want to be better? He's always gone crazy when we broke his rules or even just because he got embarrassed. In kindergarten I made him this birthday card, in Spanish and everything. I was so proud of the picture I drew, and I couldn't wait to show him. So I got home jumping up and down and shouting, 'Read it, Papi! Read it!'"

"Didn't you tell me once that he . . ."

"Basically he can't read. Not English or Spanish. But I was just a kid; I didn't know. That didn't make any difference to him. He threw my card down, walked to his bedroom, slammed the door. He might as well have slammed the door on my fingers, that's how bad it hurt."

Alan spits far into the grass. "It's not fair. You shouldn't have to suffer for his past. If it makes you feel any better, my parents think you're great. When my mom and my sister are fighting, it always comes back to what a hardworking, respectful girl you are, and why can't Jessica at least pretend she cares about her life?"

"Oh, God," I groan, *"No me lo digas.* So now I'm causing trouble in two houses. You should tell your mom that Jessica did a real good job with Anita. She's a natural."

"She liked it, too. She's going to be sad to hear that your dad nixed the idea completely. It'll be back to coming straight home after school. Like going to jail in Monopoly. Do not pass GO, Do not collect $200."

I scoot around so that we're face-to-face and twist a strand of his dark hair around my finger. "Let's talk about your family. You've got crazy shit going on, too."

Alan pulls back a little. "Why?"

"I just mean . . . it just seems out of balance sometimes, like I'm always needing and you're always giving. Maybe I should be more independent like—"

"You don't want me to help you? You don't like that I'm here for you? That bothers you?"

He asks so many questions, I can't say yes or no without saying something I don't mean.

"Forget what I said, Alan. I wasn't making sense."

"You sure?"

"Yeah. It's nothing." But when I close my eyes right now I imagine the UT campus and classes and a life all my own. Even though I know I can't do it, sometimes all I want is to get away and just take care of me.

chapter 16

"*Buenas tardes*, Papi," I say, standing up from the kitchen table and tugging Anita with me. Anita ducks her head. I wonder if he feels bad that his own granddaughter is scared of him.

"Anita, *saluda a tu abuelo*," I say.

"*Hola*, Abue," she says softly, staring at Papi's shoes. She reaches over, pats the side of his leg, and pulls back quickly.

"Did your *tía* feed you right? Is she taking good care of you?" he asks in Spanish. His eyes are trained on me.

"*Sí*, Abuelo."

"*Bueno*," he says, still staring my way, "she'd better." He pours himself a glass of Gatorade from the fridge and walks out of the kitchen.

As soon as he's gone, Anita giggles into her hand for no reason, and I plop back down into my chair.

"Let's get back to work, missy." We're making syllables by pressing mini chocolate chips into graham crackers smeared with peanut butter.

"So what about this one?" I hold up a cracker with a wobbly *c* and *a*.

"Ca," Anita says slowly. Then she bursts out laughing. "*Caca! Ca* and *ca* makes *caca!*"

"*Ay, chiquilla*, poop isn't that funny. Everybody makes *caca*," I say. I grab the cracker and shove it into my mouth. "But not everybody eats it!" I laugh through the crumbs and rub my stomach.

"Ewww," she squeals. "I'm going to tell my mom that you ate *caca!*"

"Go ahead," I say. "It's delicious."

We finish the rest of the crackers, and Anita picks up a book from our library stack. It's one of those what-do-you-want-to-be-when-you-grow-up books.

She stops at a picture of a grinning lady astronaut, a doctor in high heels, and a firefighter with a ponytail and lipstick. Anita looks skeptical. "Tía, what can girls do?"

"What do you mean?"

"What can we do?"

"You can do lots of things, Anita."

"Anything?"

I rub her chin with my thumb. "OK, anything you're

willing to work really hard for. You figure out what you're good at, and then go for it."

"And what about Mami and Abuela and you?"

I hesitate. What am I supposed to do with that question?

"Tía?" She's watching me. I'm not going to get by with some bullshit answer.

"Yeah," I say, "sometimes it just takes a lot more work than we think we can handle."

"Well, I'll be an art-test *porque* these uniforms are stupid," she says.

"Good." I pull my binder out of my bag and slide Anita's last drawing out of the clear plastic cover. "I need a new drawing for my notebook."

Anita begins her next masterpiece, and I flip through my binder. All of my old calculus notes are in here, but I haven't even bothered bringing my book home since my dad vetoed the Jessica-babysitting scheme. These days avoiding Ms. Ford at school is like a second job.

I hate to admit it, but I think Anita's little five-year-old questions might have me convinced of what Alan's been trying to tell me all along. It's time to suck it up and get back in gear. So what if UT didn't take me? I can still pass the AP calculus exam. I can still be an engineer—or something. But sitting on my butt complaining about Ms. Ford and my tough breaks isn't going to make it happen.

I pull out a piece of notebook paper and a pen.

Dear Ms. Ford,

I'm sorry for the way I talked to you after the last test. You were just trying to help me. I wish you knew how disappointed I am in myself for getting so behind in your class. I want to turn things around. But first I need to tell you a few things.

Last November, my sister's husband Jose had a bad accident at work. A forklift crushed his legs, and now he can't walk. They say it will be months before he can even try. Now my sister works at a gas station, and I take care of my niece, Anita, every afternoon.

At first I tried to do my calculus while I watched Anita because that was the only time I had. But you've got to understand that nobody, and I mean nobody, was paying attention to her. One day I just decided that it had to be me. I can't let her down. She didn't do anything to deserve all this trouble.

There's that after school, plus the job I have at Kroger at night. And since I can't work as much on weekdays, I have to take extra hours on the weekends. I cook for the family on most days because my mom doesn't get home from the bakery where she works until after 11:00 P.M.

I know you're thinking that I should explain to my parents how important this class is, how it will get me ready for college and all that. But I've been making good grades for years, and my parents still don't get why it even matters. My dad thinks that college is just a way to put off working for the family.

So maybe you can understand how I felt like there was no way to make it. But I've changed my mind. I want to pass the class and the AP exam and be ready for college math. If you help me, I think I can catch up. I'm not just doing it for me. I want my niece to see that women just like her mom and grandma and aunt *can* do hard things. I want my dad to see it, too. My boyfriend already believes it. I know you thought he was distracting me, but really he's the one who has been telling me all along not to give up.

I'm trying to think of some things that I could do to make up what I've missed in class. I have two other classes that I don't need to graduate. Maybe one of those teachers will let me go to your room instead.

Will you help me?

Sincerely,
Marisa Moreno
_____

chapter 17

It's fifth period, and I'm counting down the minutes till Ms. Ford's class, half excited, half terrified. Soon I'll know what she thinks about the letter I slid under her door this morning. When the bell finally rings, I grab my things, blow Alan a kiss, and dash out. I'm in such a hurry that when I turn the corner into the math hall I crash right into somebody.

"Easy there, Speedy Moreno," he says, grabbing my arm to steady me.

"Sorry! I wasn't paying attention," I say. I look up and see Pedro Jimenez, Jose's cousin. I guess he does know my name after all. Probably just because we were both stuck in the hospital waiting room when Jose got hurt.

I'm blushing. I tell myself it's embarrassment, but I've got to admit he's what Brenda would call "heartbreak hot." He has the kind of looks that almost make you forget you've already got a guy.

"You can bump into me anytime, Marisa," Pedro says. His smile lasts a second longer than I expect, like he wants to make sure I didn't miss it.

"Well, I—sorry," I stammer.

"You dropped this," he says, handing over my notebook.

"Thanks."

"See you later, hopefully not at the hospital." He winks and slips off into the crowded hall.

Ms. Ford is busy writing something on the board when I come in, but she pulls an envelope out of her clipboard and hands it to me. I can't tell anything from her expression. Once I get to my desk, I tear the envelope open.

Marisa,

Yes, of course I will help you. Your letter reminded me of a quote I like very much: "Don't ask for an easier life; ask to be a stronger person." Your life is far from easy, but you can use this struggle to become even stronger.

I like your idea about coming in extra during the school day. Julio from your calculus class is my teacher's assistant for third period. I can relieve him of his other duties so that he can help you go over what you need to make up. Let me know if that will work.

Your persistence makes me proud.

—Ms. F

P.S. One more thing. I was struck by how much of *you* showed in your letter. Your application essay was a fine piece of writing, but I wonder if it might do some good to send a revised version of the letter to UT. Sometimes they have a second round of decision-making to do, and if they have any sense they'll see that you have the drive to make it. And I'm telling you, that's an amazing engineering program. Sending the letter could be worth a shot. . . .

When Ms. Ford starts the class with her usual joke, I'm grinning before she even gets to the punch line.

It's surprisingly easy for me to talk my environmental studies long-term sub into letting me work in Ms. Ford's room during third period. The real teacher is still out with health problems after having her baby, and the sub isn't that impressed with the worksheets she left.

"Environmental issues?" he says. "What can this class teach you about pollution that you don't already know from living in Houston? Go ahead, you're not missing anything."

So every third period, this guy Julio from my class and I pull desks out into the hall. He re-teaches me the material I missed, and he's so patient I think he should be recommended for sainthood. And when Ms. Ford offers extra AP tutorials on Saturday mornings, I even manage to convince my manager Mr. Vargas not to schedule me to work then.

That last bit Ms. Ford wrote about UT gets stuck in my head and sets off a new chorus of maybes. Maybe a letter would make a difference. Maybe a spot in the UT engineering program can still be mine. Maybe it's not too late. Maybe . . .

I spend three lunch periods in a row applying online for financial aid, glad for once that I've been stuck helping Ma with the taxes for ages. I also type up a new letter based on what I wrote to Ms. Ford. I don't say anything to anybody, not to Ms. Ford, not to Brenda, not to Alan, but a few days later I mail it off to the same address where I sent my UT application.

March

chapter 18

Alan drops me off at school on Saturday mornings for the tutorials with Ms. Ford on his way to work out with the baseball team. I leave the house in my Kroger clothes, even though I don't go in to work until one o' clock, because it's the easiest way to keep my dad from grilling me about where I'm going.

Today we park at the front lot closest to Ms. Ford's room. Her car isn't here yet.

"Hey, I have a present for you," Alan says. He reaches behind the seat and pulls out a package wrapped in Sunday comics.

"What's this for?" I ask.

"Today's the third."

"But my birthday isn't until August third."

"No," he says. "The third month we've been going out. Good excuse for giving a pretty girl a present."

I tear into the wrapping and pull out a blue T-shirt screen-printed with a ketchup bottle. The label says "Butterfly Brand Catch-up, the #1 Calculus Condiment."

I hold the shirt up to my chest. "I love it. I can't wait to show it off. Ms. Ford is going to crack up."

"She'll get the butterfly thing?"

"Oh yeah, one day after school Brenda even told her that shit story Cecilia made up about my parents almost naming me Mariposa because of my stupid birthmark. What a load of crap—I *wish* it was shaped like a butterfly."

Ms. Ford still isn't here, so I slide over next to Alan and fit myself against him. We start kissing and don't stop until we hear Ms. Ford's car pull into the parking lot.

———

It's 11:30 at night when my manager finally locks the doors at the front of the store, and I can feel the long day in my sore back and feet. I'm cleaning the last register when he comes out of his office and walks over.

"How was everything today?" he asks.

"Busy, like always," I say. I lean down to scrub a sticky spot on the grocery belt. Mr. Vargas gives me the creeps, and I don't like to look at him. "How are you, sir?"

"Fine," he says. "You know, your dad came by today."

"He did?"

"Came by this morning."

"Looking for me?" I pretend to be focused on a non-existent stain on the side of the register. I'm already wondering what kind of pissed-off Papi is going to be when I see him next.

"Yeah. He seemed to think you'd be working the morning shift, too."

I look up. "Well, you know I used to—"

"He was real surprised when I told him you wouldn't be in until later." Mr. Vargas frowns. "I thought you needed the time off so that you could help out with your family."

"On the weeknights I have to take care of my niece. That's why I've been trying to pick up extra hours on the weekend."

"Just not in the morning? We always need morning help on Saturdays."

"It's because I've been going up to school for tutoring," I explain.

"Really," he says without much interest.

"I was pretty behind, but I'm catching up."

"Huh," Mr. Vargas scratches his head. "As long as you graduate." He cares more about fast scan times than he does about good grades. But every time I get finished with the tutoring with Julio or Ms. Ford, it's like I'm reclaiming a little something for myself. The work is hard, seriously hard, but not like a double shift here at the store. It's hard in a way that makes me feel like I'm on my way.

Maybe I don't know exactly where I'm headed, but at least I'm moving.

"Thing is," Mr. Vargas says, "I mentioned something to your dad that I've been meaning to talk to you about."

"Yes, sir?"

"You know, if you could commit to more hours, you'll make head cashier in no time. We're looking to hire at least two more so that we can have a head cashier on the floor during every shift. You'd get to be in charge. Manager's assistant, basically. There's a pay increase, too. Two bucks more an hour."

I can just see my father salivating at the thought of the extra money. "How many hours are you talking?" I ask.

"Thirty, thirty-five a week."

I drop my rag and stand up. From somewhere in the back of the store the whirring of the floor-waxing machine comes up. "I'd really like to, Mr. Vargas, but I've got to get through this semester. Just a couple more months. Then I can do it. It's just that right now I'm stretched pretty thin."

He looks disappointed. "Your dad didn't think there'd be any need to wait around."

"I'll think about it, but I just don't see how I could."

"Well, I need to know soon. I guess I'll have to ask someone else." He starts to walk away.

I go back to cleaning, then remember my paycheck.

"Mr. Vargas?"

"Yes?" He stops and looks all excited.

"Could I grab my check before I forget it?"

"Stop by the office when you're done cleaning. And think about the position. It's a good opportunity."

Half an hour later, I'm tired, hungry, and cranky from waiting for Gustavo to pick me up. When he called back after my text, I heard laughter and music in the background. I'm not going to lie, it gives me some satisfaction that he has to leave a party to come get me.

Gustavo weasels out of jobs at home, never pulls his weight. Just about the only thing that's changed for him since Jose's accident is that he has to drive me and Mami around a little more. And that he drops his car and truck magazines off at Cecilia's so that Jose can look at them. Wow, what a sacrifice.

The employee lounge is just a big closet with hard chairs and a rickety table. I cross my arms on the table and lean forward to put my head down, but the envelope in my back pocket digs into my butt. I pull it out and rip it open.

After taxes, I made $160. I think back to when I used to make twice that much, before I had to drop so many hours to take care of Anita. I crumple the envelope into a ball and stuff the check back in my pocket. Like always, it'll have to do.

chapter 19

Sunday's another long day—first Mass with Mami, then a double shift at Kroger. I've got that gritty, end-of-the-day feeling that won't come off no matter how many times you wash your hands.

Alan and I both just got off work, and we're unwinding over ice cream at McDonald's. In the booth behind Alan there's a bunch of boys, maybe twelve or thirteen, snickering and elbowing each other. I lean to the side to see what's so funny. Big mistake. They're squeezing ketchup out of packets and making designs with it on the table. Gross. Alan glances over his shoulder and shakes his head. "No home training, I guess."

Then he launches into a round of impressions of the customers who came to the restaurant where he busses tables. He puts me into hysterics.

"Do the rancher again, please," I say when I can talk again.

He shakes his arms out, then pulls his eyebrows down low over his eyes and hunches his back a little. "Hey kid, you go tell Loopy that I want one of them puffed-up tortilla thangs. What you call it, a soapy pillow? Gwon now, kid."

I can barely breathe I'm laughing so hard. "No way this guy can be that ridiculous, I mean *de veras*?"

Alan scoops a bit of strawberry goo up in his spoon. "I think everybody's pretty weird if you're paying attention. And what else am I going to do while I'm stacking plates and wiping up globs of salsa?"

"What if you did cartoon portraits, like the ones at carnivals?"

"You mean where they make your head gigantic over a tiny little body?"

"Exactly. Give people something to remember El Ranchero by."

"Jimmy'd never go for it. But I sort of made money off my art today."

"Really?"

"Remember that drawing I showed you the Monday we didn't have to go to school?"

"The one of Jessica?" I remember it perfectly.

"A while back this guy in my graphic design class said I should show it to Mrs. Green, the advanced drawing teacher, so I did. Well, she asked to scan it, said she'd see what she could do with it. I figured, why not?" Alan shovels in the last of his sundae.

"And what happened?"

"So Mrs. Green called me today, and the drawing won a prize, a partial scholarship to this design school here in Houston."

"That's amazing!" I hop up from my side of the booth and scoot onto the seat next to him so I can get my arms around him.

"I didn't know I could do anything like that," he says. "Not until you made me think of it, back when you got into U of H. I'm going to fill out the FAFSA, see if I can get some financial aid because the program costs way more than the scholarship. But it's a start, you know?"

I think about the UT application I mailed out months ago and the wishful-thinking letter a few weeks back. I would have heard by now if they were going to take me. It looks like there won't be any big start for me at UT, no Marisa-on-her-own fairy tale.

"I know, baby," I say. "A start is everything."

⸻

Mami is sitting at the kitchen table with a mess of bills spread out in front of her. There's a faint burned smell in the air, like maybe the pot of *frijoles* on the stove boiled over earlier.

I kiss her on the cheek, pull out my wallet, and slide eighty dollars onto the table. I've been giving up half of my paycheck so long that she doesn't even have to ask.

The lights are off in my parents' bedroom, but shadows from the TV flicker on the wall. I can just make out my dad sitting in the middle of the darkened room, a bottle in hand. I'm praying he'll stay there.

I slip out of my work clothes and into a T-shirt and jeans. I'm feeling responsible, so I stop to pick up some dirty clothes and papers off of the floor before I go back into the kitchen to help Mami.

When I come back out of my room, I see that my dad is at the kitchen table, too. Great. He holds up a bill and frowns at it like he can read it.

I pretend not to notice and start pulling out what I need to get dinner ready. I'm measuring the rice when Papi calls me over.

"*¿Es todo?*" he asks pointing to the four twenty-dollar bills fanned out in his hand.

"That's half, Papi," I answer in Spanish like always. "You know how I had to cut back my hours to help Ceci with Anita during the week."

"Every time, it's less that you give us. What used to be $150 turned into $100 last time, and now just $80? You have a responsibility, *mija*."

"I know, Papi."

"This Mr. Vargas said you could get as many hours as you want."

"How can I watch Anita and work at *el supermercado* at the same time? I work whatever shifts I can, but I can't put extra hours in the day." I think for a second that my mom might back me up, but she just stares down at the table.

"Mr. Vargas said you quit working Saturday mornings," he says. I can feel how hungry he is to catch me lying.

"It's because of my grades. I was falling behind in some classes and I needed to go up to school for extra help, and—"

"Or so that you could run around with that *desgraciada* Brenda. And your *novio*." He spits that last word out like it leaves a bad taste in his mouth, even though he's never even bothered to talk to Alan. "We need at least $75 to pay for the gas bill. And $45 to make the payment on the credit card."

"But that'd only leave $40 for me. I gave you half already," I say. I try to keep my voice calm, but inside I'm screaming in protest. I used to save for college every month, but lately it's impossible.

"Are you part of this family?"

"It's just that next year I'm going to have school to pay for—"

He slaps one hand hard against the other. "*No importa.* Worry about that later. Right now we need to pay the gas bill."

I chew on the inside of my cheek, but I just can't hold myself back. "Does Gustavo give more than half?" I say. "And does he take care of Anita for two, three hours every day?"

Mami finally looks at me, her eyes flashing a warning. But I don't stop. "That is half, Papi."

"It's not enough." He crumples the wad of bills and tosses it onto the table.

"Oh, OK. *Qué tonta*, what was I thinking?" I grab my wallet out of my backpack and pull out the two fives that are in it. I slap them down and then unzip the wallet's side pouch. A rain of coins clatters over the table. I shake the wallet to prove that it's empty.

"Is that better, Papi? Is that what you want?"

"You'd better be finished, *hija*."

"I don't know, are you satisfied? Or should I find something of mine to sell? Maybe just quit school altogether so I can work as many hours as you want?"

"Marisa!" my mom gasps. Her hands shoot up to the crucifix hanging from a chain around her neck.

I fold my arms over my chest so Papi won't be able to see how badly my hands are shaking. I've never crossed him like this.

"*Ingrata*. You will do your part."

"I am, Papi, I already *am*," I say. "I swear I do my best. I watch Anita, I cook, I work at the store, I don't complain, I—"

"Call Mr. Vargas. Ask for more hours."

"Omar," Mami starts to say, but Papi ignores her.

"Marisa." He points at the telephone.

"I can't take on more hours. I have to keep up with school, and I need the tutorials on Saturdays."

"You need to act like the daughter you were raised to be." The vein in his forehead pulses blue.

I turn my back to him and start chopping an onion, an onion for his supper. An onion like a thousand others I've chopped before. I watch each row of tiny white cubes fall before I make the next slice.

Then I get an idea. I set down the knife and reach into the drawer where I stick all the report cards my parents have ignored over the years. I cross the room with a handful of them. "Look. See this?" I thump the top report card. "See these?" I say, fanning the rest right in front of Papi's face. "These are almost all A's. The best grades. The highest. They are worth something, at least to other people, they show how hard I work in school."

He doesn't look at the report cards. He just points to the phone again.

"It's nothing to you, I guess. I'm *nada* to you, one big nothing. I get it." I start to rip up the cards.

"Now are you finished?" he says when I drop the papers in front of him. He grabs my arm and puts his face close to mine. "We need you to help with the money. You will work more hours."

His hand feels like a steel band on my arm, and I can smell the beer on his breath. "What about you? What if you stopped drinking? That would free up some funds."

Now I've really done it, said the thing nobody's supposed to say.

He stares straight at me. "I am ashamed that you are my daughter."

A muffled cry comes from Mami.

"*Cállate*, Patricia. Her ingratitude is worse than anything she could do. This girl is not the one we raised."

When he says this, a new wave of anger crashes over me. I turn away, wondering what to do, where to go. I grab my backpack and run to the door. It's cold outside, but I can't go back for my jacket now.

"*Mija*, don't," Mami says. Her face makes me think of a crumpled paper bag.

"Let her go," Papi says. "She can come back when she is ready to be a true daughter."

chapter 20

I hunch against the cold and tap on the window. A gust of wind blows through the backyard, rustling dry leaves against the steps. I shiver and knock again.

"Alan!"

Finally I hear movement inside and Alan opens the door to his bedroom.

"Hey," he says, squinting at me. "You OK?"

I shake my head.

"Come here, baby." He eases me inside, and I'm crying before he even sits me down on the bed. He holds me close and leans back so that we're nestled together against the wall. He strokes my hair with one hand and rubs my back with the other.

"What happened?" he asks softly.

"My dad . . ."

"Did he hurt you?" Alan's voice gets hard.

"He said . . . *cosas tan feas*. And I made it worse, I—I never should have said . . . I didn't think. I can't go back now."

I bury my face in his pillow, which is soft and cool against my hot cheeks.

"It'll be OK. I'm here, I'm here," he whispers.

He stays close and talks to me like that until I fall asleep.

When I wake up a few hours later, I wish I hadn't. Everything I've tried so hard to do is gone like some stupid sandcastle swept away with one wave. I swear I'm done wanting a life that'll never be mine.

What I want is to stop thinking, to be real in my body and free from my mind.

I want to feel that I'm not alone.

I pull my T-shirt off so that when I lie down next to Alan, I can feel skin against skin. Then I slide my hands up the leg holes of his boxers. I close my eyes and pretend I'm Brenda. I pretend I'm beautiful and funny and totally in control as I start to touch Alan. I close my eyes and move my hands gently. It's working, working like magic, erasing Mami and Papi and my report cards and Kroger.

Until Alan wakes up.

His eyes open extra wide, and his mouth does, too. He stares at me and blinks, like maybe that'll make me disappear. So I tug down his boxers to prove that this is real and so am I. I'm lowering my head when a feel his whole body tremble. His hand shoots out and stops me.

"Marisa, no," he says. He pulls my hands away from where I'm touching him.

"I want to," I say. "What's wrong with that?" But I already know what. I'm not Brenda, not beautiful.

He shifts his boxers around, digs for my T-shirt, and throws it over my chest.

"You don't want me," I say. I curl up on my side and start to cry.

"That's not true." He hugs me stiffly, like I'm a crazy person he doesn't really want to be close to.

"Then why not?"

"You're upset; you're not thinking straight."

"I'm thinking fine! You're my boyfriend; I want to be with you." I start to move back toward him. *Let's just do it,* that's what I'm thinking.

He wraps his arms tighter around me so that I can't move. "I don't want you to have regrets. You're too special to me for it to be like this."

"I know what I want. You just don't understand me." My voice is getting louder, but I can't help it. "I feel, I feel like I've got nothing to hold onto. I need you." Now I'm crying into the wall. "Please, I need you." When his arms relax a little, I try to turn and put my body against his the right way. I want him to hold me like my boyfriend, not like a straightjacket.

"Don't, Marisa," he says. He stops me again. "I know that things have been bad. But I'm here, and I promise it's going to be OK."

I don't know what the hell he's talking about. I want to scream. If he wants to, he can make it OK right now. He could hold me, touch me, tell me he loves me.

"I need to feel you." I press against him again. The hardness is still there. His body wants me, but he doesn't.

"It's not the right way," he says, "Later we can talk, but try to think. I mean, think about Ceci—and Jess . . ."

"I don't want to think!" I yank my body free of him and shove him. "Why are you playing with me? I thought you understood me, I thought you wanted . . ."

"Not like this."

"I hate you," I hear myself whisper. I pound my fist against his chest. "I hate you!"

Alan grabs my hands and stops me from hitting, but he doesn't try to hug me anymore. "Shhh," he says.

I clench my teeth and press my body back against the wall. I lie there, not moving, until Alan falls back asleep. All the anger in me is gone. All I can feel is how alone I am, even with Alan beside me. I needed him to make me forget, to use his touch to erase everything. But he doesn't want me.

I've got to get out of here.

I wait as long as I can. When I count to a hundred twice without hearing Alan's breathing change, I tiptoe to the door. I don't turn around to look at him.

I stumble out into the backyard, shoes and backpack clutched in my arms. Partway down the block, I sit on the curb and pull on my tennis shoes. There's no music, no shouting, no dogs barking. My world is going to hell, but the neighborhood is perfectly quiet. I want to scream.

Instead, I dig out my cell phone. It's 2:10 A.M. My fingers shake when I call Brenda.

"Please pick up," I whisper into the darkness.

She does.

"Sorry, I know it's late," I say.

"Shit, forget that. What's the matter?"

"Everything." I can barely squeeze the word out past the tears. "It's . . . I had to leave my house."

"Where are you?"

"On Alan's street, near the corner. Can you . . ."

"Stay right there," Brenda says. "Give me ten minutes."

I'm still sitting on the curb when Brenda drives up. I feel dizzy and queasy when I get up, like somebody just kicked me in the gut.

"What happened?" Brenda's eyes search my face.

"A fight with Papi, and then . . ." I start crying again.

Brenda tries to get me to come home with her, but I don't want to talk about anything, not today, not tomorrow, not ever. I just keep telling her to take me to Ceci's, and finally she does.

I wave good-bye, then walk up to my sister's apartment. I slip my fingers around the right key, then hold the rest carefully so they don't make any noise.

Once I'm inside, I ease my backpack to the floor and find the couch with my hands. I've never wanted so badly to disappear. I bury my head in my arms and fall asleep with my shoes still on.

chapter 21

The nonsense chatter of cartoons wakes me up. When I groan and roll over, Anita jumps up onto the couch.

"Tía Marisa!"

"Hi, *chiquita*." My voice comes out in a croak, and my mouth is so dry I can't even lick my lips.

"What's wrong with you?" Anita looks me over. "You sick?"

"Yeah, I guess so. Is your mommy up?"

"Nope, just me."

I sit up. I want some water, but first I reach out to Anita. I know she won't turn me away.

She wraps her arms around my neck and kisses my birthmark. "*Oye*, Tía, *sabes qué?* I can make my own breakfast."

I go to the kitchen and get my glass of water. I also find out that Anita's "making breakfast" means getting the Lucky Charms out of the cabinet.

We snuggle down in front of the couch and watch an hour's worth of PBS cartoons. Anita picks the marshmallows out of the cereal and complains about not getting to see *Dora the Explorer* on Nickelodeon. I try not to think about anything.

"Marisa?" Cecilia is standing in the doorway of the bedroom she shares with Anita now. "What are you doing here?"

"Hi, Ceci," I say, getting up from the floor. I try to smile.

Cecilia gives me a questioning look then bends down to hug Anita. "Go get dressed. I'll check on you in a minute."

Anita closes up the box of cereal before running back to her bedroom. Breakfast is over.

"What the hell happened?"

"I had a big fight with Papi. I can't go back," I say.

"Shit, I thought it was my job to be the screw-up daughter. You're supposed to stay on his good side."

"I guess those days are over. Now he thinks I'm a disgrace."

"Welcome to the club," Cecilia says, yanking my ponytail. "But being a bad girl is no good for you. You look awful."

"Thanks."

"Sorry, but it's true. What are you going to do?"

I play with a Pop-Tart wrapper on the coffee table. Last night I couldn't think past finding a place to sleep. Now I know there's no way I can face Alan at school.

"Can I stay here for a while? You could call Mami before she comes over, tell her I can watch Anita today. Give her a break."

"You're not going to school?"

I poke at a ripped spot in the carpet with my toe and ignore the question. Who is Ceci to give me a hard time about cutting one day of school?

"All right, I know I owe you," she says finally. She sticks her head into the kitchen to look at the clock on the microwave. "Damn it, I'm running late already. Look, I'm worried about you. We're going to talk for real tonight, got it?"

I nod.

"I'll call Ma." Cecilia hugs me and then digs the phone out from between the couch cushions.

Before she leaves, Cecilia explains Jose's schedule. A nurse comes at 10:30, and today is his day to go to the physical therapy center at 1:00.

"They'll come and pick him up; they even put him in the wheelchair and take him to the van. Other than that, you can pretty much just ignore him. He sleeps all day anyway, and the nurse takes care of his pee bag. All he really needs is lunch. Ma usually brings him something when she drops Anita off next door, but he can eat whatever." Ceci tucks her Stop-N-Go shirt into her black pants with one hand and grabs her purse with the other. "Anything else?"

"I'm fine," I say.

"Let's make lunch for Daddy!" Anita tugs on my arm.

We just got done with the nurse. Before that we read about fifty books and made a whole stack of houses out of cut-up construction paper and tape. I'm tired, but I say OK.

"You pick the menu, *chica*."

"Hmmm ... apples and marshmallows and Kool-Aid?" she says.

"Let's add some quesadillas to that, and it's a deal."

Anita sprinkles cheese on tortillas, and I slice the apples. Even with my hands busy, my thoughts keep drifting. I can just see Brenda running up to Alan during lunch, all worried and full of questions. What will he say? What does he think of me now?

We put the food on a tray, and I'm halfway through the living room with it when Anita stops me.

"What about dessert?" she frowns. "*No tenemos* dessert for Daddy."

"You already have marshmallows," I point out.

"Tía! Marshmallows is a vegetable."

"Who told you that?"

"I know, a pudding!" she runs to the fridge and comes back with a little plastic tub and a spoon. She sticks them both on the tray. "Now we're ready."

Anita opens the door to Jose's room and I start to cough. It smells like he just finished smoking his tenth joint. But she doesn't seem to notice. She slides easily around the medical equipment everywhere and climbs onto a box so she can kiss him without jostling his bed.

"How's my beautiful girl?" he asks, his voice raspy. Every time I see him, I'm surprised all over again by how different he looks. He used to keep his body built up, but now his arms and chest are super thin. The worst bruises are still healing, and his face is shades of pale yellow and green, the way people look on TV when you mess with the color balance. His eyes are sunken and watery, and he hasn't shaved.

"We made you lunch!" Anita says. She runs over to me and picks up the glass of Kool-Aid. "It's cherry, the best kind."

"Thanks, baby," he says. "You know what? Daddy really wants one of his silver cans from the fridge. Be a good girl and go get one for me."

Anita's face falls a little, but she carries the Kool-Aid out.

"I'll drink it," I shout. "I love cherry." I give Jose a look. "You don't got to be such an ass," I say when Anita is out of earshot. I put the tray in front of Jose and help him elevate the top half of the bed. "You want a beer, let me get it for you."

"Back off, OK? The last thing I need is another bitch telling me what to do."

I start to talk back, but he raises a hand.

"I'm not trying to get into it with you, Marisa, I'm just saying. I hear it *cada día* from Ceci; I hear it from your ma; I hear it from the damn nurses. *Por favor*, just give it a rest."

Anita comes bouncing back in with a can of Coors Light.

"*Qué te dije* about how to carry those?" he says when he sees her. "Now I got to wait a long time or it'll spray everywhere."

Anita's smile vanishes. "I can get you another one."

"No, that's OK. Just walk next time, for Christ's sake."

"I put you some pudding on the tray, Daddy."

"It looks good, baby." His face softens. "*Dame otro beso aquí.*" He touches his stubbly cheek. She climbs back up on the box and kisses him.

"Now go find something to do so me and your *tía* can talk for a minute."

"Listen," he tells me a second later. "Sometimes I have a visitor or two in the afternoon."

"OK."

"I got that physical therapy thing today, so if anybody comes for me, all you got to do is open the door. And don't say nothing to Cecilia."

I lean down and pick up some empty beer cans from under the bed. "I don't think your bad habits are that big of a secret, Jose."

chapter 22

By the time we finish with lunch and get Jose packed off in the physical therapy van, I'm exhausted. There's not much good aunt left in me.

"How about a nap?" I ask Anita.

Her whole face wrinkles up. "I hate naps."

"Not for you, just for me. How about you keep me company so I can fall asleep? After that, you can do what you want."

Like always, Anita takes her job of putting Tía to sleep so seriously that she's out cold in minutes. I'm sinking into my own dark cloud of no-thinking when a knock at the apartment door pulls me back. I ease out of the bed and smooth the covers over Anita.

I look through the peephole and see Pedro Jimenez, Jose's cousin, the same one I crashed into in the hall. He jiggles the doorknob like he expects the door to be open, then knocks again.

"Hang on," I say. I flip the lock and open the door. He's standing there with his hands in his back pockets. He wears ordinary jeans and a button-down shirt, but they fit like they were designed just for him.

"Hi," I say.

"Marisa? Didn't expect to see you here."

"No school?" we ask at the same time.

"Jinx," Pedro says, laughing. "I guess we don't need to make excuses to each other. And I thought you were Ms. Model Student."

"I guess not." My neck feels warm, and I realize that I'm blocking the doorway. I step back. "Coming to see Jose?"

Pedro walks into the living room. "Yeah, I've got something for him. He should have something for me, too."

"Maybe he left it for you in his room. You can go check, see if you find it. He won't be back from physical therapy until later."

While Pedro is in the other room, I fiddle with the edge of my shirt and sit on the couch with my knees pulled up next to me. I dig around in my backpack, ignore my cell with its five messages, and pull out the novel I'm supposed to be reading for English.

A minute later, I look up and see Pedro watching me.

He leans against the doorway to the hall. "You look cute when you're reading."

I blush. "Find what you were looking for?"

He sticks his hands back in his pockets. "Nope. Needed it, too. I guess I can talk to him later."

"I'll tell him you came by," I say. I get up to open the door for him.

He doesn't move. "Or I could just wait till he gets back. I've got nowhere to be."

I hesitate. Part of me finds it hard to believe that he has nothing else to do. But another part of me thinks anything is better than an empty living room where I'll be alone with my thoughts.

"You want to hang out? They don't have cable," I warn him.

"I don't feel like TV anyway," he says.

"OK. Make yourself at home." I sit back down. I'm still holding the book.

He steps closer and leans over my shoulder. "So what you reading?"

I close the book and tilt it so he can see the cover. "*Things Fall Apart*, it's for Mrs. Garza's class."

"Damn, girl. You do homework even when you're skipping? That's messed up."

"Like I said, no cable."

Pedro sits down on the couch and reaches for the book. "Chin-u-a A-che-e-bee," he sounds out the author's name. "Somebody's mama didn't like him very much. Does old Chee Bee put things back together?"

"What?"

"You know, *Things Fall Apart*. Maybe he should go to technical school so he can put them back together."

I surprise myself by laughing. "Maybe you should go to technical school so you can repair your sense of humor."

"Hey, you laughed," he says.

"I guess I did."

"So what's falling apart in the book?"

"I don't know; I barely started it. But I'm guessing it's the kind of stuff nobody can fix."

"Like Hyundai SUVs?"

I roll my eyes, but I can also feel a little bit of tension easing out of me. "Probably like family problems."

"You like it? I mean, would you read it even if you weren't trying to get a good grade in Mrs. Garza's class?" He tosses the book back to me.

"Probably not. I've got plenty of problems of my own, don't really want to read about more."

"Yeah? What problems have you got?"

I don't say anything at first because I think he might still be teasing. But Pedro watches me, waiting, until I feel like I've got to say something.

"It's just—I've got a lot I'm supposed to take care of." I shift the book from one hand to the other. "A lot on my mind."

"I'm a good listener," he says. He pulls his knees up to his chest and wraps his arms around them like a little boy pretending to behave.

"Now you're making fun of me."

"I'm not shitting you. Try me out." He rests his chin on his knees and smiles at me.

Something in the gesture turns a key inside me, opening me up to him. I set down the book.

"My dad and I had a big fight. Over grades."

"You got bad grades?"

"Nah, I'm trying to get good ones. That's what's got him mad, sort of." It sounds even crazier out loud, and I laugh. I mean to stop right there.

"Go ahead, tell me about it. You might feel better."

I bite my lip and feel my hand drift up to hide my birthmark. It's either start talking or start crying. So I babble about my mom and Cecilia and Anita and Ms. Ford and UT and the tiny Kroger paychecks and my dad and how even my boyfriend thinks he knows what's best for me.

Through it all, Pedro nods and watches me with solemn eyes. And when I do start crying again, he's no longer this serious little boy listening on the other side of the couch. He's right next to me.

"Don't cry all by yourself," he says. "Come here." He offers me his arms.

I let him hold me, and he smoothes my hair almost like Alan does. I pretend that I'm where I belong, that I'm safe and wanted. I know that this is all wrong, but it's like that feeling you get when you're standing at the top of a staircase, looking down, and all of a sudden, you just know you're going to fall. And, more than anything, you *want* to fall. The only thing that stops it from happening is that you look away for a second, and when you look back down again, the spell is broken.

But when Pedro pulls my face toward his, I don't look away. I see what he wants, and I want it, too. I think for half a second about how long it's taken me to climb to the top of the stairs, how hard it was. And in the other half of the second, I decide to see how fast I can fall.

He slides his lips over mine and opens my mouth with his tongue. The first thing that I notice when he starts kissing me is that his mouth tastes like cigarettes, but also like tortillas and oranges. The second thing I notice is how different it feels from Alan's kisses.

I push the thought away and kiss Pedro, sliding my hands up his arms and around his shoulders. He pulls me in tighter. I can feel his whole body wanting me. His hands drift down to my waist and then up under my shirt, unhooking my bra.

Pedro's hands are cool and strong and fast. My body's right there with him, throbbing under his touch. That bad-girl damp heat is between my legs. But there's something else, too, a feeling like a sob gathering in my chest. When Pedro starts kissing me again, it feels all wrong. No matter how hard I pretend, he isn't Alan.

"Hey, hang on," I say, trying to slip out of his arms.

"Shhh, you're just nervous." Pedro's hands are on my thighs, and he presses his face toward mine. I twist away.

"No, no—I really don't . . ."

"Come on." He turns my face back toward his. "Just relax. This is what you want, you know it is."

His tongue is back inside my mouth, and his hand closes around one of my wrists. My heart is pounding out a distress signal. *Stop it Stop it Stop it Stop it.* My eyes close. In the dark of my mind, I can still hear Alan whispering, "It's not right." But there's no way back to Alan as Pedro presses his face into the hollow of my neck. No way back now that it's Pedro's breath hot and damp against my skin. Then I know the truth: I'm getting exactly what I deserve. This is what I wanted.

But it's not what I want anymore. I almost cry out, but then I think of Anita in the next room.

"Stop, Pedro. I don't want to do this," I say as loud as I dare.

"You don't mean that. Just let yourself go."

"I do mean it, I . . ."

"Just shut the fuck up, you started this." He squeezes the inside of my thigh so tight that I can still feel where his fingers were even when they slip away and start yanking down the zipper of my jeans.

Right then I shove Pedro in the chest with one elbow and yank myself over to the other side of the couch.

"What the hell?" he says, glaring at me.

And then he's right on top of me, undoing his belt and pants. He's pinning me down with his hips, and the feel of him against me is too real, everything is too real. I keep thinking of Anita, of Alan, of everything that makes this so wrong, and how it can't be happening but it is. I'm crying now because I don't know what else I can do.

"Don't, please don't. Stop!" I beg. I push him again, but I know that I'm not strong enough, that if he wants to he'll . . .

And then, all of a sudden he's off of me. I open my eyes and see his hard cock inches from my face, but he's already pulling his pants and boxers back up. Like he's not going to do it, like I'm safe. The tears come harder.

"Stop crying, you little bitch. Save yourself if that's what you want." He zips his fly and fixes his belt, shaking his head. "You're a fucking cock-tease, you know it?"

I scramble to fix my jeans and pull my shirt down as far as it will go, but I don't say anything. I don't trust myself to even try. I just cross to the door and open it. I can hear laughter from the parking lot, then a car door slamming. I stare at the apartment opposite Cecilia's.

Pedro walks over to me. I can feel him inches from my face, his breath on my skin. The heavy scent of his cologne makes me want to gag. I glance up and then wish I hadn't. His face is flushed and his mouth is twisted into a sneer.

"You think you're different, but you're not. In the end, you're still a slut on the inside," he says. He grabs my breast and squeezes it hard. And then he's gone.

I lock the door behind him and curl up on the floor, hugging myself and crying. When I finally get up and go to the bathroom, I don't look in the mirror; I just drop my head straight over the toilet and throw up until there's nothing left.

I turn on the shower, dying to scrub every inch of my body, but then I hear Anita moving around in the next room.

"Tía?" she calls from the hallway.

"Coming!" I shout through the door. I shut off the water and yank my clothes back on.

"What's wrong, *chiquita*?" I ask, opening the door and kneeling down by Anita. I try to sew up all the darkness I feel inside a smooth face and steady voice.

"I had a bad dream," Anita whispers, twining her fingers into my hair. "Somebody was hurting you. I thought it was real." Her cheeks are splotchy and damp from crying.

"Oh, *mi corazón*, sounds awful. But it was just a dream. Come on, let's chase that dream away." I guide her back into the bedroom.

I grab a Disney CD from a pile on the floor and shove it into the yellow CD player I bought her for Christmas.

"Aladdin," Anita says, already humming along with the music.

"That's right. OK, I need you to be a really big girl for me. I need you to stay right here and listen to Aladdin while I take a bath, OK? Your Tía Marisa is still feeling a little sick. Can you do that for me?"

Back in the bathroom, I turn the water on as hot as I can stand it, and then a little hotter. If I can just wash everything away, maybe no one will ever know. But it doesn't matter. Because I know what I wanted to do, what I almost did.

When the hot water runs out fifteen minutes later, I don't even realize it until my teeth start to chatter.

"Marisa!"

Cecilia shakes me awake, and my first thought is of Anita. But I open my eyes and see that she's lying on the floor next to me, perfectly safe. We're watching *The Little Mermaid*.

I sit up. "How was your day?"

"Shitty, but not as bad as yours, looks like. You're going to ruin your skin crying all day. Let's talk."

She pulls me into the bathroom and sits me down on the toilet. "OK, what's going on? Out with it."

"The fight with Papi," I say. I blink the sleep out of my eyes and pull my fingers through my damp, tangled hair.

"How'd it start?"

I tell her what happened, up to when I walked out. My voice sounds far away to me, like I'm reading to her from a newspaper. Yesterday feels like forever ago.

"Why do you let Papi get to you? I mean, I know he always does, but, you know." She stops and leans closer to me. "That can't be all."

"I . . . Well, when I left the house, I went to Alan's. I thought he would make me feel better, but he didn't."

"*Hombres*," Cecilia says, shaking her head. "They're never as good as they seem at first. *Nunca*." She pulls a brush out of a drawer under the sink and hands it to me.

I thank her and start working through the knots in my hair.

"So did you guys have a fight?"

"Sort of." I shrug. I should tell the truth right now so that Cecilia doesn't get the wrong idea about Alan, but then I'd have to go back and explain everything I did. So I just drag the brush back through my hair and avoid my sister's eyes.

"That just proves it for sure," Ceci says.

"Proves what?"

"That you're better off without a guy, at least for now. Shit, the last thing I want you to do is end up like me."

"You're doing OK. Anita's pretty awesome."

"Yeah, sure, but my life's a mess. You're going to be the one who really does something, you know? So don't let Papi or Alan or nobody slow you down. What's it you want to be, an electrician?"

"An engineer. I mean, I think I do."

"Right. You're going to college *y todo*, and that's that. No back talk."

"OK, Ceci. Thanks." It comes out shaky, but I look at her and smile. Inside, though, I'm thinking of Alan, and how I wished I'd listened when he tried to slow me down.

Cecilia pulls me up from the toilet and spins me around. Half a minute later she's got my hair in a perfect, sleek ponytail.

"How about I go pick up some ice cream for us?" she asks.

Back in the living room, my sister paws through her purse, pulling out wadded papers and discount cards. "Nothing," she says. "You got a ten, maybe?"

"Nope, I threw it all at Papi."

"Right." Cecilia looks around the room like the money might sprout from the stained carpet. "I'll look in Jose's room," she says finally.

When she comes back from the bedroom, Jose's shouting after her, "That's my cash!" But the edge of his voice is softened by the pot he must be smoking.

"Just be glad I didn't take your stash, too!" she shouts back. She turns to me. "Idiot doesn't even bother to hide that shit."

"Cash . . . stash . . . That rhymes!" Jose laughs like crazy. Then he remembers that he's angry. "Bring my money back, *puta*! Bring it back!"

"Yeah? Get up and make me, asshole!" Cecilia kicks the door to his bedroom shut.

"It never ends," she says. "Look, you hang out with Anita, and I'll be back with the ice cream." She kisses Anita on the top of the head and grabs her purse.

I close the door behind her. When I turn back around, Anita is still staring straight ahead at the TV. She looks stiff, and I realize now that she didn't move once during the shouting match between Cecilia and Jose. She's watching that movie like it's the only thing in the world.

"Baby," I say softly, squatting down beside her.

She stares at the TV.

"Did you have an accident?"

She droops a little. "*Lo siento*, Tía. I didn't mean to."

"It's been a tough day for everybody, baby. Let's get you changed, then I want you to pick out a book."

We curl up in Anita's bed to read, both of us trying to ignore the dark things at the edges of our minds.

chapter 23

"You OK?" Brenda reaches over from the driver's side to hug me. "How come you haven't been answering your phone?" she says. "I've been worried as shit, *chica*. Alan, too."

She's got this look like she's not going to drive us to school until she gets an answer.

"I was sick," I say. It's sort of true. The thought of answering my phone, reading my texts . . . it made me feel like puking. I just couldn't face what anybody had to say.

And I still can't. Here I am sitting next to my best friend, and there's no way I can tell her what happened, what I did. At least not any part that matters.

Brenda squeezes my hand. "Did you call your mom or anything? About the fight?"

"I've got to figure out what I'm going to do first."

"Just tell me whenever you want to, you know, talk about things," Brenda says. "And whatever happened with Alan, I know he just wants you to be OK."

"I just need to think."

"Sometimes you think too much, girl." Brenda slides her hands around the steering wheel and finally backs out of the apartment complex.

I stare out the window, squinting in the too-bright morning light. Everybody at school is going to take one look at me and know. Slut! Cheat! Liar! And then the thought of seeing Alan—I can't. I've got to keep him away, at least for now. I pull out a piece of paper and write a note.

"Do me one favor," I say a few minutes later as I fold the note. "Give this to Alan for me?"

"Give it to him yourself. You know he's going to be waiting for you in the cafeteria."

"I can't, not today. Got to go straight to the calculus sweatshop." I try to sound like the same old Marisa.

"Fine, I'll give it to him." Brenda holds out her hand and takes it. For once, she doesn't press for more information.

When we're pulling into the student lot, I grab my bag and start to open my door before she parks.

Brenda pulls over to the curb. "OK, eager beaver." She smiles at me, but her eyes are worried.

"I'll be in Ms. Ford's room." I shrug my backpack onto my shoulders and swallow back the sick taste that comes up in my throat.

Ms. Ford frowns as soon as I walk in and points at one of the chairs by her desk. "Go ahead and sit down. You need to see your score from Friday's practice test."

Perfect. The last thing I need is more bad news.

"You've got to know, it's awful." She sighs and hands the test to me.

I unfold it slowly. Before my brain can process what's there, Ms. Ford starts laughing. "Awfully amazing!"

Across the bottom of the exam, it says in huge letters, "YOU PASSED! THIS WOULD BE COLLEGE CREDIT ON THE REAL AP EXAM!"

"You're sure?" I turn the test over like it might have a failing grade on the back.

"Sure as sure." Ms. Ford takes a powdered donut from a box on her desk and offers me one. "You're a little weak on the multiple choice section, but you and Julio aced the open-response questions. I knew you could catch up."

I blink, thinking of the T-shirt from Alan. Butterfly Brand Catch-up. I don't think I can ever smile again. I hand the test back to her.

"So, uh, I—I just want to know what I missed yesterday and Monday," I say. My face feels hot, and there's not enough air in this room.

"Only a review of the exam. I'll give you a copy of the answer explanations. What's wrong? You should be proud." Ms. Ford comes to my side of her desk and studies my face.

"Your sister?" she asks in a you-can-trust-me voice.

"I really don't want to talk about it," I say. I can't look her in the eye, so I stare at her pale, freckled arms.

"Sometimes not talking just makes things worse."

She wants a story, I can tell, but there's no story for me to tell. Just black feelings balled up inside me.

"Excuse me, miss." I don't wait for her to say good-bye. I have to get out the door before I start crying.

When the first period bell rings, I'm still hiding in the last bathroom stall. It's the closest thing to privacy in a building with three thousand other people.

Somebody bangs on the stall door. "What the hell are you doing in there? Painting your toenails? I got to piss."

I clear my throat. "Sorry, not feeling too good." I hold my breath until the tardy bell rings, and the bathroom empties out.

I slide down the wall and pull my knees up to my chest. My head aches, and my breathing is ragged and full of tears. I press my cheek against the cool tiles, not even caring if they're dirty.

I don't want to think about anything, but when I close my eyes I see the note I wrote to Alan.

Alan,

Sorry for Sunday night. Please don't call me. I know you'll understand. You always do.

—Marisa

---

chapter 24

"Seriously, I'd let you stay longer," Cecilia says, flattening her hands against the kitchen counter, "but the last thing I need is one more strike against me, *sabes*? Papi's had time to cool down. He probably doesn't even remember what happened."

"Yeah, right." We both know that Papi holds grudges like they're gold.

"Well, anyway, Ma misses you *mucho*."

"Don't worry about it. I understand," I say. For once, Cecilia's in the position I usually get stuck with: trying to help without getting pulled down into the mess.

"I called Gustavo, and he's going to pick you up from work tonight."

"OK." I focus on the sandwich and spread the mustard all the way to the edge of the bread. Just like in the commercials. I stack the turkey and cheese on top.

"Look, I hate to bring this up, but can you keep Anita tomorrow?"

"Of course," I say. "Thanks for letting me crash here and everything."

"What matters is that it's all OK now. And no more fights with Papi. I'm telling you, you will be *jodida* if you don't get your little butt into college. I will personally kick your ass." She grins and takes a bite of my sandwich. "But it's kind of cool to know you're not a total saint."

———

I have to close at work, so it's already late when I walk out into the parking lot. Gustavo's truck is in one of the first spaces. I open the door and climb in.

"Hey, sis," he says. "How are you?"

"How do you think? Sunday was rough."

"I know what you mean," Gustavo says.

Like hell he does. He fiddles with his stereo, rolling through all the FM stations before sliding in a Tejano CD I hate.

"What are you waiting for?" I ask because I don't know what else to say. But if he wants to sit in the parking lot all night long, fine by me. I'm in no hurry.

"Just wanted to talk. Pops, uh, he hasn't said a thing since you've been gone. Just been hiding out in the bedroom and staying late at work."

Staying late means drinking at the bar next to the welding shop where he works.

"And Mami?"

"She told me about the fight. It sucks, but you know how Papi is. You've just got to do what he says. Give him a little more money if that's what he wants."

"Easy for you to say. I can't help it if I haven't been able to keep the same hours at work. My free time goes to taking care of Anita. By myself. Don't get me started on that, Gustavo. You haven't exactly been my hero lately."

"Yeah, yeah, yeah," he says. "That thing about not working Saturdays, just so you can go to school even more, it's . . ."

"Not something you would do, I know. But I actually care about school. And I am working Saturdays, *pendejo*, just not in the morning." I cross my arms.

"You make such a big deal about that stupid math class. You graduate in a month. Why sweat it?"

"You wouldn't understand." I stare out the window and wish I could just zap myself straight into bed. I don't want to face my mom, or worse, my dad.

"Don't be pissed at me, Marisa. I'm just your *tonto* Tavi."

I bite my lip. I haven't called Gustavo "Tavi" since we were little. I swear I'm not going to cry.

"We kind of figured something out, Mami and me," he says. "I'm going to give you forty-five bucks a week to give Papi with your check. I already worked it out in my head. I just have to do one extra transmission a week. No big thing."

"You're serious?"

"I mean, it's weird to care so much about school, but you've always been weird. And maybe that's not such a bad thing. Anyway, after you graduate, you can fend for yourself. But for now, Ma's going to help, too. Remember those napkins she used to make with Tía Elena? *Para bodas*? So there's this wedding planner that buys cakes from the bakery, and she said she'd pay Ma twenty bucks for *cada* set of eight. That extra money goes to you, too, so you can pay Pops more without giving up your school stuff."

"But Mami never goes against him."

"She wants you to come home."

I stare at him because I don't know what to say. Then I lean over and hug him like I am five again.

"*Familia* takes care of *familia*. We're going to make it," Gustavo says.

———

"Here, *mija*, your favorite," Mami says the minute we walk into the kitchen. She puts a pineapple empanada on a plate and motions me to the table. I thank her, but I sit for a long time just staring at the pastry. The only sound is Mami sliding her crucifix back and forth on its chain.

"*Mira*," she says finally, "your papi is not a bad man." She leans toward me, and the shadows under her eyes seem darker than usual. The whole kitchen looks dingier, too. Then I realize it just seems that way because Gustavo finally replaced the burnt-out lightbulb over the table.

"I know he's not." I break off a piece of empanada and nibble it. The sweet filling turns my stomach, but I don't want to hurt her feelings.

"Sometimes things from his past make it so that he acts bad *sin querer*. He doesn't mean to hurt us, it just happens."

"It sure felt like he wanted to hurt me," I say to the empanada.

"Gustavo told you about our plan?" Her voice brightens.

"*Sí. Gracias, Mami*. It means a lot that you want to help me. Makes me proud to be who I am." I talk fast because I don't feel proud at all. But that isn't her fault.

"It will get us through for a while, *pero* I've been thinking maybe being around your father is not so good for you."

"What do you mean?" I study her face. All I see are worry lines and the tiny hairs growing out of the mole by her ear.

"Your papi, he's not going to change," she says. "You are a good daughter, *mija*, but . . ."

"I don't know what else to do, Ma. I just want to pass my AP calculus exam and graduate ready for college. *Pero después*, I can work sixty hours a week if he wants. I can . . ."

"You won't need to. You won't have to worry about your papi anymore," Mami says. She lets go of her crucifix, and her fingers drift to the wedding band on her left hand.

"Mami?"

"*Sí, mija?*"

"Are you . . . are you thinking of, you know, divorcing Papi?"

"*Por Dios, no!*" She crosses herself. "*La iglesia nos enseña—*"

"I know what the church says. I just thought—OK, forget I said that. So how are things going to change?" I pick at the empanada a little more.

Her voice comes out soft and low, almost pleading. "You need to settle down with that Alan. *Es un buen hombre, mija*, a really good man."

The bit of pastry in my mouth turns to chalk.

"He's ready, *mija*. He just wants to take care of you. You finish school soon; you could have a summer wedding, start your own life. *Imagínate*, you won't have to be here with your father anymore."

"Where's this coming from, Ma? He's not— We barely started dating!"

"The best for you is to be away from here a little. Your father will always be too hard on you."

"It doesn't work that way, Ma. No way we're ready to get married. Alan doesn't even . . ."

"He's ready, *mija*."

"What makes you think that?"

"He came here Monday. He said you didn't come to school. *Ay, cariño*, he was so worried about you."

What am I supposed to do with this? *Now* I find out that when I thought he never wanted to see me again, he was here making plans with my mom? Why didn't he come find *me*, come tell me that everything was OK between us? Why didn't he come to Ceci's instead of Pedro?

But these questions are pointless because I've already screwed everything up. Nearly got screwed. There's no way for things to be OK now.

"If you stay here, your father will keep making things hard for you. *No es justo*, but that's how he is." She's talking fast now, like maybe she can tell I'm getting lost in my own thoughts. "Just hang on a little, and then Alan will be the one in charge."

"Come on, Ma. He only thinks he means it. And anyway, I'm the one who's in charge of me."

She gives me this sad smile that says she's sorry I'm so confused about the world and why can't I see the solution in front of me? She puts her hand on my arm. "OK, *mija*. Eat a little more and go to bed. You'll see things different tomorrow."

"Maybe," I say. I just want to go to my room. I force another bite of empanada and kiss her good night.

I thought I'd feel better back in my own bed, but instead I feel like there's a giant pit inside me, and I'm about to get sucked into it. I get up and pick Paco up from where Anita left him in the corner last time she was here. I lie back down and wrap my arms around his soft teddy-bear belly. The dizzy, sick feeling comes back, and I squeeze my eyes tight against it. I try to pray for sleep. And when sleep doesn't come, I pray for forgiveness. And when the guilt doesn't go, I pray to forget.

April

chapter 25

"You've got to take it," Brenda whispers. "He made me promise I'd put it into your hands."

I shake my head, but I let Brenda slide the envelope over to me. I can't open it. Alan thinks he knows what happened, and maybe he can forgive me for the way I acted at his house, but there's no way he can forgive what I did with Pedro. It would only hurt him to know.

I scribble across the envelope and pass it back to Brenda.

She stares at the block letters of my one-word reply: SORRY. Our government teacher starts giving instructions for a project, but Brenda snaps her fingers until I look her way. She points at the letter and mouths, "What the hell?"

"Later," I mouth back.

"You can't expect me to give him this," Brenda says after class.

"Please, Brenda."

"I'm going to open it if you won't."

"If it'll make you feel better," I say.

"What would make me feel better is for my best friend to tell me what's wrong! The boy you used to be crazy about has been trying to talk to you, but you just push him away. You won't respond to his texts, you ignore his calls, you return his notes without reading them. So you didn't want to spend the night at Alan's after the fight, whatever. But what happened?"

"Sometimes things happen that are better not to talk about," I say. I want her to understand that I don't want to hurt anyone, that I'm trying to hold back the hurt.

"I love how you trust me *so much* to help with your problems," Brenda says. Her sarcasm feels like a slap.

"I'm sorry," I say.

"Stop saying that! You're always sorry, but never sorry enough to do anything. It doesn't make sense. What's up with you?"

When I don't say anything, Brenda grabs her bag and throws it over her shoulder. "I guess I've got to give this 'treasure' to Alan. Awesome. You know that Jimmy benched him because he can't think straight enough to play baseball? He's going nuts over this. Look, don't expect any more favors from me." She turns away from my desk and walks out of the room without looking back.

I just sit there. I should be running after her, trying to patch things up, but the thing is that I'm scared to be in the rush of people in the hall. I can't stand to feel all those bodies move against me. I don't want anybody to touch me. Because there's no way to know what they're thinking, what they would do to you if there was nothing to stop them.

"Can I stay here for lunch, miss?"

"Again?" Ms. Ford looks up from her desk. "Don't you ever eat in the cafeteria?"

"Please," I say.

"You know where the problems from old exams are. But you can't hide out here forever."

I don't need forever, just until school is out. She can't say no today, anyway. I'm not the only one coming for extra help during lunch. Everybody's cramming for next week's AP exam.

I pull a problem sheet from the table scattered with handouts and sit down at a desk by the wall. I put a hand on the window. Everything is green and new outside, but I don't feel anything. There's the warmth of the glass against my skin, but it can't get inside me where everything is frozen. Mrs. Garza made us read this poem in class that said "April is the cruelest month." Everybody else thought that was stupid, how was a month going to be cruel? But to me it makes perfect sense. It's cruel because the whole world turns pretty and green while everything in your life is going sour. And you can't blame anybody but yourself.

Calculus is the only thing that can make me forget how messed up I am. The numbers are always the same, always predictable, always safe. The magic works until the bell rings.

I'm gathering up my books when Ms. Ford points to the door. "Somebody's waiting for you."

———

"You can't keep doing this to me," I say.

"Can you hear yourself? What about what you're doing to me? You've got to talk to me. Please, Marisa." Alan reaches out for my hand, but I take a step back.

"You only think you want to talk. Shit's happened that you can't even understand. It's—"

"Who says I won't understand? You're the one who doesn't understand. I'm ready to support you."

"I've heard all about how ready you are," I say. I guess I'm really loud because a couple of people down the hall turn to stare. I lower my voice a little. "My mom told me about your little visit. Don't you know me better than that? I don't want to get married, not right now."

He puts his hands up. "I know that was a bad idea. I just felt so freaking useless seeing you get torn up by your dad again. I wanted to help."

"So you proposed to my mom. Great solution."

"Come on, Marisa."

The tardy bell will ring any second. I have to act fast to get him to go away and stay away for good. It hurts to be this close to him, to be reminded of what I threw away.

"You think I need rescuing? You think you can fix everything? You go around me to my mom like this is some nineteenth-century novel or something. Having my mom breathing down my neck about getting married is the kind of help I don't need, trust me."

Alan's face goes so sad now that I just want to reach out and touch him. But it's too late to go back. I already ruined what we had. He just doesn't know it.

"How can I make it OK?" Alan asks. There's still a flicker of hope in his eyes.

"It's over, Alan."

"I know you don't mean it, Marisa," he says weakly.

"Yes, I do." I stare him in the eye and try to make my voice like steel. He has to believe that this is the only "I do" he'll ever get from me.

"You aren't—this isn't like you." His brown eyes are wet now.

"Maybe you just didn't know me," I say as the second bell rings.

"Please, Marisa."

"Better hurry up, we're already late."

"Don't do this."

"Good-bye, Alan," I say. And I leave him standing there. I walk until I get to the end of the hall. Once I'm around the corner, I run. Past the economics class we're both supposed to go to and up the stairs. I can't let him see me cry because then he might guess that the last thing I want is to be away from him.

But when I get to the upstairs bathrooms, I stop short.

Pedro Jimenez is standing in front of the water fountain with his arm around Brenda's shoulders.

chapter 26

"Look," Pedro says to Brenda, reaching out to wrap his other arm around me. His smile brings everything back. "Your friend can vouch for me, we're cousins by marriage. I'm a nice guy, right, Mar?" He squeezes my shoulder hard.

I want to shake his arm off and push him away, but I'm paralyzed. His cologne is the same.

"Who said I was looking for a nice guy?" Brenda says. She smoothes her hair and sweeps it over one shoulder. "You got a brush, Marisa?" she asks, already tugging me toward the bathroom. "Later, Pedro," she says over her shoulder.

"Come see me when you want some trouble," he calls to her.

"Not a word," Brenda hisses once we're in the bathroom. "No lectures, OK?"

"What about Greg? I thought—"

"Let Greg take care of himself. He's been spending way too much time around that girl from the tennis team. Way too much time. Like I haven't noticed." She punches the button of the hand dryer for emphasis.

"What?" I shout over the dryer. "He's totally into you, Brenda, you know that."

"Jesus, Marisa!" She walks over to the mirror and smoothes her eyebrows.

The dryer shuts off, but Brenda's voice is just as loud as before. "Stop taking everything so serious. It's time to have some fun. Not everyone wants to spend their last month of senior year moping around in some math teacher's room."

I flinch.

"You and me always talked about senior year, what a good time we'd have. *Pero* you haven't even bothered to hang out with me or anybody for ages." Brenda crosses her arms.

"*Es que* . . . I just haven't felt like myself."

"If you say so," Brenda says. "But it's not like you're the only one with *problemas*. I miss you, Mari. You act like you don't care about anything. You walk right by the lunch table without saying 'hi,' you never call me back; what am I supposed to do?"

"I'm sorry. I've been a crappy friend," I say. "So catch me up. What's going on?"

"Just exploring new territory," she says. She pushes herself up onto the edge of the handicapped sink and swings her legs.

"You broke up with Greg?"

"Not exactly, not yet."

"But don't you owe it to him to—"

"Wait a second," Brenda interrupts. "Don't you be telling me what I owe Greg, OK? Look what you did to Alan! He's *loco para ti*, and then all of a sudden you just decide to ignore him. No explanation. No way he deserves that."

"Maybe it's me, not him."

"Well, he sure as hell don't know that. And so what if it is just you? I can say that, too. It's me, not Greg. There. Will that get you off my back? I just want to have some fun, *comprendes*?"

Normally I would back off, but I can't let this go, not now that Pedro's in the picture.

"It's not even about that. Have your fun, *no importa*. But Pedro Jimenez, he's—"

"Damn hot," Brenda says. "And he's got the best connections for parties. *Lo mejor.* Come on, Marisa. We're only seniors once. This is it. You've got to get out and enjoy it while it lasts."

"But what if—"

"What if nothing. *Ay, Marisa.* We have got to get you out of this rut. You talk like you're thirty years old, and you're barely going to turn eighteen. What you need is a good party. Pedro told me about one next weekend. All the seniors who—"

"No," I say. It makes me feel sick just to think of being anywhere near him. And it would be even worse to see him with Brenda. "I can't."

"What is your deal?" she snaps.

"Please, can we just stop talking?" I close my eyes and start to tremble. I need to get away fast because a big wave of sadness is coming, and it's going to hit me soon. But there's no time.

The tears run in straight lines down my face.

"God, Marisa, don't cry. Forget what I said, I didn't mean to be so damn nasty." Brenda squeezes me tight. "Don't worry about it, OK?"

"But I am worried," I whisper into her shoulder.

May

chapter 27

"Ma, if you still want to go to Mass, we have to leave soon," I call.

It's Wednesday afternoon, Mami's day off. She talked Gustavo into watching Anita so that we can go to Mass and light some candles before tomorrow's AP calculus exam.

"Mami?"

"*Sí, mija*, I'm just looking for *mi rosario*." Her voice is muffled, and I can hear her going through her drawers in the bedroom.

I stand up from the kitchen table. "Did you check in here? It's probably with your other church stuff." I pull open a drawer and sift through layers of prayer cards and Sunday bulletins.

As I'm pushing aside a copy of *Oraciones para Madres/Prayers for Mothers*, something catches my eye, an envelope at the very back of the drawer. I slide it out and see that it's got my name on it, and it's postmarked February 26.

My heart is pounding. I don't know what I feel more of, excitement that this letter came for me at all, or anger that it was kept from me. I'm still staring at the unopened letter when my mom walks into the kitchen.

"I found it." She holds up the rosary. "What is that, *mija?*" she asks. She slips her reading glasses on.

"When did this come?"

"That? Ay, *no sé.*" She hesitates and rolls the rosary beads between her fingers. "I meant to tell you about it, *mija*, but things got so crazy. Plus you were busy with Alan and taking care of Anita—"

"Come on, Mami. Why did you hide this from me?"

"I wasn't hiding it," she says. "*Es que* I just didn't want—"

"It's addressed to me." I tap the envelope. "Marisa Moreno."

"*Mija.*" Mami puts her hands together like we're already in church. "*Dime*, does Veronica Gomez ever come home to see her family? She wasn't even at her brother's wedding. Yolanda says that she barely calls."

"Vero joined the army, Ma. She's stationed in Germany. Of course she can't just come home whenever."

"I just knew it would be the same for you. How could I make it without you, Marisa? I need you here, helping me.

The family needs you. College is good, but you could go here. Houston's good enough, isn't it?"

I turn the envelope over in my hands.

"I've been praying for you since forever, *mija*, wanting good things for you. But if you leave, you won't come back. And then what will I do? And what about *la chiquita*?"

That is so low, dragging Anita into this. Mami even reaches onto a shelf by the stove and takes down my favorite picture of her.

"Nobody can take care of her like you," she says.

I start to tear the envelope open.

"*Mija*, please don't." Mami lays her hand on the letter.

I pull it away and hold it against my chest. "You've already tried that, Mami. Go ahead, go on to Mass without me."

"Please, Marisa," she says. "The letter doesn't even matter. Don't you want to be with Alan and stay with your friends? There are colleges right here."

"I'm going to open it now." I slide my finger all the way under the flap of the envelope.

"After everything, sometimes you can be so ungrateful!" Mami says all of a sudden, but she doesn't move. I can feel her looking over my shoulder.

When I refold the letter, I look up and see that she's crying.

"Oh, Mami," I say.

"The main thing is that they accepted you," Ms. Ford tells me the next morning. She lowers the letter to her desk and picks up her breakfast taco.

"But the response date already passed. What can I do now?"

"There must be something. Let me check into it, I still know a few people at the university."

"OK, miss. But I—"

Ms. Ford waves my words away. "You just worry about the exam today. Good luck!"

In the testing room, I line up my pencils and look around at the other kids from my class. A few people look so nervous they should have a puke bucket by their desks. But my calculus buddy Julio just grins. I know he's thinking that we are so ready for this.

There are plenty of questions I don't understand. I skip them like Ms. Ford taught us to and finish all the ones I do know just before time is called for the first section. The second section even goes a little better than the first. When the test proctor calls time, I almost can't believe it. A year, practically a whole year of work, and it's over just like that. I kind of feel like when you fall asleep in a movie and all of a sudden the credits are rolling, and you don't know what the hell happened. You don't know if you liked the movie or hated it or if you wasted your ten bucks. And there's no way to figure it out because it's already over.

I have ten minutes before lunch, so I do the only thing I can think of and wander down the stairs to Ms. Ford's classroom. I tap the window on the door and wait for her to look my way. When she does, I give her two thumbs up. She tells the class something, then comes to the door.

"You look pleased," she says.

"Yeah, it went pretty good, I think." I want to say more, like ask her about this one question on derivatives, but we're not allowed to discuss anything on the exam for forty-eight hours.

"Listen," Ms. Ford says, "the dean of the College of Engineering is supposed to call me back later today. I'll keep you posted on anything I find out."

"Thanks, miss."

I'm walking away from Ms. Ford's room when I hear Brenda's footsteps behind me. I know it's her long before she gets close.

"Boo!" she shouts, grabbing my shoulders from behind.

"Yikes!" I say, really making a show of it. "Seriously, Brenda, I don't think you've actually snuck up on me since middle school."

"It's hard to be sneaky in heels," she admits. "So? How was it?"

"Not bad. I think I might actually have passed. Sucky thing is we don't find out until July."

"Not to freak you out, but it's usually the tests I think I did good on that I end up failing."

"*That's* reassuring."

"You want some French fries? On me?"

"OK," I say. And then we're walking together toward the cafeteria, almost like nothing was ever wrong between us.

chapter 28

"I'm going to read *todo esto*," Anita says, holding up a picture book.

"OK," I say. I pull her into my lap. I'm lucky to get away with it. Lately she's five going on fifteen.

"Mar-tin was mad," Anita begins. She doesn't go on until I give her a smile. "Mar-tin was mad and sad. Mar-tin was mad and sad and also lone . . ."

"Sound it out, *chiquita*."

"Also lone-lee."

"Good girl."

I try to focus while we read the rest of *Martin's Mess*, but my thoughts drift. Things are OK with Brenda as long as I don't think about how "friendly" she's become with Pedro. But I miss Alan so bad.

It's like Anita can read my mind, because when she finishes the book, she asks, "How come I don't see Alan *nunca*?"

"*Es que* . . . I hurt his feelings."

I jump up to kill a roach that's creeping along the wall opposite us. I hope she'll forget about Alan by the time I get back from flushing it down the toilet.

"Did you say sorry like Martin?" Anita asks.

I sigh. "Things in real life aren't always like in books, Anita."

"Like hell!" She jumps up and puts her hands on her hips.

"Anita! Don't say that."

"Mommy does."

"Well, it's a word for grown-ups, not little girls."

"So are you going to say sorry like you're 'posed to?" The bossy look on her face makes her a very convincing miniature of Cecilia. I almost laugh.

"It's *not* funny." Anita gives me a long, disapproving look, then scoops up the book again and moves to the edge of the couch, as far away from me as she can get. She flips through the pages slowly, a determined look on her face. She stops on one page, following the text with her finger and mouthing the words, then thumbs forward a few more pages. Finally she holds the book up with the pictures out toward me, like she's the story-time lady at the library. "Read here," she says.

I scoot a little closer to her. "OK. It says, 'Martin was not mad anymore. Now Martin was just sad. Will Grandma ever love me again? That was what he wanted to know.'"

Before she turns the page, Anita carefully shows the pictures to me and to the stuffed animals she lined up on the couch earlier. Martin, the overweight teddy bear, is standing outside his grandmother's house, apparently too scared to knock.

Anita taps the first word on the next page.

"Grandma came outside and told Martin how happy she was to see him."

Anita shows the pictures and turns the page, and I read on.

"'You aren't mad at me?' Martin asked. 'I'm sorry for breaking your vase.'"

"Grandma told him that she forgave him already. She was just waiting for him to come see her." In the picture, Grandma hugs Martin.

"Keep reading!" Anita says.

"Martin knew what it was like to be mad and sad," I read. "But he knew his favorite way to be was GLAD. And that's just how he felt when Grandma forgave him. The end."

Anita closes the book. "*Now* you going to say sorry?"

I half nod, half shrug.

"If you don't, you're going to be really sad. And I'll be mad." She brushes her bangs out of her eyes and gives me her best grown-up look.

"We'll see, Anita," I say.

"So you'll make Alan glad again so that *el padre* will call you man and wine at church and I can be the flowered girl?"

She doesn't miss a thing. I ignore the "man and wine" bit, but she keeps at it until finally I text Alan to see if he'll meet me before school tomorrow. He doesn't respond until much later when I'm already in bed, and even then it's just a one-letter text: "K." But I'll take what I can get.

chapter 29

I don't know what to do with myself while I wait for Alan under the oak tree. I'm nervous and excited, hopeful and scared, plus a half dozen other emotions I don't really have names for. Basically, I'm feeling everything all at once.

I lean against the tree and try to imagine how things were, that easy closeness between us. I close my eyes and let the good memories and the warmth of the morning draw me in.

"Marisa."

I open my eyes. "Alan!" When I try to hug him, he steps away. I think about all the time separating us from the last night we were together. The way I've acted, he has a right to be mad.

"I brought you Krispy Kremes," I say, pulling the box of doughnuts out of my backpack.

Alan barely glances at it. "Not hungry, thanks."

"Oh, OK." I drop the box and sit back down by the tree. "Do you have time to talk?"

"I guess." He hesitates. I think he's going to sit cross-legged by me, like always, but he doesn't. He sits down more than an arm's length away and turns his body at an angle so that he isn't really facing me. He picks at the edge of his sketchbook.

"So?" he says.

I know it's my job to start this conversation, but I don't know how to crack through the awkward silence. And with the way he's sitting, I can't even see his eyes. I feel like I'm talking to his shoulder.

"I miss you, Alan."

"It's been a while," he says flatly.

"The way things have been between us, it's not what I wanted. You've always been there for me, and I—"

"That's right, I've just *been there* to you. Off to the side. Not important. Disposable."

I think of Anita's little book and its easy apology. I was stupid to think a few words could make everything up to him.

"I'm sorry, Alan, I—I messed up so bad I don't know where to start."

"Maybe with the part where you stopped speaking to me without telling me why?" he says. He hunches over a little and starts shading something in his sketchbook.

"I felt so ashamed. I just didn't know how to face you."

"So you kept things simple and dumped me? *Muchas gracias.* You're too kind."

"No, I know I should have explained, but I . . . something else . . ." What am I going to say, I felt so bad, and while I was at Cecilia's . . . ? Or, maybe I sent the wrong signals, but I didn't mean to . . . ? It was an accident, but I almost lost my virginity to another guy?

"I'm sorry." I scoot closer to him, like maybe that will make this easier.

"Don't," he says. His back stiffens.

I slide back again, but not before I see what he's drawing.

"Like it?" he says, tilting the sketchbook toward me. "You were the inspiration."

In the middle of the page, there's a brick wall, half built. On one side of it, in the foreground there's a girl huddled against the wall like she's scared of being seen. Dark tears stream down her face, and in the V of her shirt, a heart wrapped in barbed wire is visible. Blood trickles down where the barbs press into her skin. Around her, piles of bricks wait to be added to the wall.

On the other side, there's a rough sketch of a boy. He's slumped against the same wall. The ground around him is littered with crumpled papers. Just under his shirt you can see his heart, almost covered over in bricks. His tears fall into a pool around him, and ink from the crumpled-up letters mixes with them, forming the words SHUT OUT.

"I'm sorry, Alan," I say again. I don't know what I'm thinking, maybe that the third time will be a charm and he'll forgive me.

"You can't just take things back. You say you're sorry. Well, that takes down one brick. But there's still a whole damn wall. What can you do about that?" His voice is shaky with emotion. "You never even read the letters that I sent you, never even bothered."

"I thought it would be easier if I didn't try to see you, I thought there was no way you could forgive me. If you knew . . ."

"Are you joking? How could you think that even for a minute?" He turns to face me. His lips are pinched tight, and a muscle jumps just above his jaw.

"I was so confused by everything, the fight with Papi and then . . . I just couldn't . . . I just can't . . ." I stammer.

"I know something happened, OK?" His face softens a little. "I don't know what, but I've known you long enough to know when you're keeping something back. *¿Y porqué?* When have I disappointed you?"

"Some things just mix everything up. I got mixed up, and I thought you would hate me. But I could try to—"

"Don't bother. Because now I know *que no me conoces.* After everything, you don't know me at all."

"I do, Alan, I do," I say, almost begging now. "I was wrong for how I treated you. I know that. I was just so afraid."

"Well, you can't take it back now just because you changed your mind. You tore my world apart. I could take anything as long as I knew I had you. Jessica's problems, my problems, your problems, I could handle it all because I knew at the end of the day we were together. Then you just . . . I thought you loved me like I loved you."

"I did, I promise. I still do." And when I say it, I know just how much I love him. And at the same time I feel how I've already lost him.

I thought that I could find my way back into the circle of his arms where everything is possible, where I know who I am. But that stupid hope turns out to be just another dead-end street.

"Even I have a limit," Alan says. He picks up his sketchbook and closes it. "You don't need me, Marisa Moreno. You'll be fine on your own."

I sit with the ants creeping over my legs and watch him walk away.

I pull myself back together by the time school starts. What I want to do is just quit the day and go home to cry, but this is my life now. I can't keep pretending it's going to get better on its own.

I have to do something about it, starting with this whole Brenda and Pedro thing. I scan the tables in the cafeteria and see him, but Brenda's not with him. At least that's something. Everywhere I look lately they're together.

Then I see Greg leaning against a pillar and fiddling with a carton of chocolate milk.

"Marisa!" He gives me a little wave.

"Hey," I say, walking over. "How are you?"

"Been better, I guess." He tosses his milk carton into the trash.

"I'm sorry," I say. I hope it means more to Greg than it did to Alan.

"You mean about Brenda?" he asks.

"Yeah." I'm glad he's the one to bring it up. "That really sucks."

"You know how she is." He rubs the toe of his shoe over a black scuff mark on the linoleum. "I mean, I know her, too. I just had this dumbass idea that I was special and it wouldn't go down with us like everybody said it would."

"What'd she say?"

Greg shrugs. "It was all a big excuse. Some crap about how we've got to explore because it's—"

"Senior year," I finish for him.

"Exactly."

"She told me the same thing. I tried to talk sense to her, but once she gets an idea, that's not easy."

"Thanks. It's no big deal," he says without meeting my eyes.

"Don't take it personally. Anyway, she might still come around. I'll keep working on her."

The bell rings, so we say good-bye and head in opposite directions for our classes. When I walk into government, instead of sitting in my usual desk toward the front, I find Brenda at the back of the room.

"Hey," I say.

"Hey yourself," she says. "How's the schoolgirl?"

"If we're going by my last progress report, the school-girl is officially in hiding. But me, I'm fine."

"Saw you talking to Greg. What's up with that?"

"Just trying to cheer him up. He seemed pretty low. You had a good thing going with him."

"Yeah, yeah, yeah. So sweet, good guy, I know. But I want to have some fun. Just fun. You could get in on the action, too."

The teacher hushes everybody and starts writing down the averages from the last three tests and explaining the extra-credit opportunities. A few minutes later, Brenda slips me a note:

Look, let's make a deal. How about you come with me to a party this weekend, and I'll have a real talk with Greg? It's a perfect trade. And I swear if you ain't having fun, we'll leave the damn party. So check one . . .

❏ **I'm willing to let a little adventure into my life. I'll go with you to the party Friday.**

❏ **I'm a total chickenshit, and I'd rather do calculus homework and pick my nose.**

---

chapter 30

"It's a party, Marisa. Just let me give you a little more mascara."

I have to move fast to get out of Brenda's reach. "I already feel like my eyelashes weigh a ton."

"Let's see." Brenda pulls me over to her full-length mirror. "Damn, we're hot," she says. She straightens the edge of her tight black skirt and then blends my eye shadow with her finger.

"We do look pretty delicious," I admit.

When I came over earlier, Brenda tossed me a bag with this pink tank top covered in sequins. At first I thought it was way too much bling for me, but looking at my reflection, I'm OK with it. Against the pink, my skin looks kind of like toasted almonds. Maybe I don't feel quite like myself with all the makeup on and everything, but this night isn't about me.

I'm still looking for some way to talk to Brenda about Pedro. But we've been having such a good time, almost like the old days, that I don't want to ruin it. Anyway, I've got all night. As far as Mami and Papi know, I'm sleeping over at Cecilia's to babysit.

There's a knock at the door, and Brenda's dad sticks his head in. "Bren? We'll be home, so you're gonna call us if you need a ride back from the party, got it?"

"Got it, Pops," she says. She stands up on top of a stack of textbooks so that she can give him a kiss on his very shiny bald head. "We'll be good, don't worry."

"Smart choices," he says. "You're the only baby we've got."

"Bye, Dad," Brenda says, scooting him out the door. "Love you, be back before two, promise!"

She's smirking when she turns back toward me. "He'll be *totally* dead to this world before midnight. Poor old man." Brenda checks the time on her phone. "It's almost eleven. The party should be going by now. You ready?"

Really, I'm not, but I nod. "Just got to find my sweatshirt." I paw through the pile of clothes on Brenda's bed.

"No freaking way!" she says. "You are not covering that sexy tank top with a dumpy sweatshirt. Just suck it up. We're in Houston, it's barely even cold outside."

"I guess I'll have to sing to stay warm."

"God, no!" Brenda groans, but I'm already croaking out a dangerously off-key version of "I'm Bringing Sexy Back."

"Spare me." Brenda tosses me the sweatshirt. "You can wear it in the car, just stop singing."

All the way to the party, Brenda talks about Pedro, what he told her about the party, how funny he is, his body.

I tell myself that I need to wait for the right moment, but I can't stand it. "Watch out for him, Brenda," I say finally.

"Look," Brenda snaps, "don't even start. I just want to go to this party. And who made you the judge anyway? Just because Pedro is Jose's cousin don't mean you know everything about him."

She doesn't say anything else until we pull onto a street lined with parked cars. "Just chill. And take off that lame-ass sweatshirt."

"Look, I didn't mean—"

"Don't worry about it," she says, rolling her eyes. "Relax a little." Brenda slicks on a little more lip gloss and checks my makeup.

Music blares from the house, and some guys smoking on the porch whistle when we walk up. I follow a little behind Brenda, wishing I'd never agreed to come along. As soon as we're inside, she dances into a group at the center of the living room. "Come on," she shouts.

I shake my head, suddenly embarrassed. My hands are damp, and I stand by the wall pretending to enjoy the music. Mainly I'm watching out for Pedro. I don't want to get caught anywhere near him, and I don't want Brenda to either.

After a few songs, Brenda shimmies away from the other dancers and crosses over to the drink table. A minute later she hands me a plastic cup full of something that looks like thick red Kool-Aid.

"Try this."

"Thanks," I say with enthusiasm I definitely don't feel.

"Look, I know I said we'd go home if you weren't having fun, but you have to make an effort. Get off the wall and dance. A little of that liquid courage in you and you'll do fine." Brenda slurps the last of her drink.

I tip back the cup. "It's good," I lie.

"Down it and get out here!" Brenda shouts as she starts dancing again.

I'm finishing the drink and moving away from the wall a little when I see Pedro come in. He grabs a beer and slips in with the dancers. Within minutes he's dancing close to Brenda. I stare at her and will her to turn away and dance with somebody else, but instead she raises her arms and moves with him. His hands go everywhere.

You'd think I'd have a plan for dealing with this, but it turns out that I don't. I take a step back and then head for the door, squeezing past the people standing along the wall as I go.

"What's your hurry, *guapa*?" a tall mustached guy calls when I get to the door. "Come dance with me."

I shake my head and push past him. The front porch is empty except for a couple dozen cigarette butts scattered on the floor. One of them is still smoldering, and I grind it out with the heel of my shoe. I take some deep breaths.

The bass from the speakers inside makes the wooden porch shake a little, but it's quiet here by comparison. Across the street, somebody is watching *Saturday Night Live* in the dark. A cool breeze rustles through the pine trees alongside the house. I cross my arms over my chest and try not to think about Pedro dancing with Brenda. I'd give anything for Alan to be here with me, for things to be the way they were before. He'd know what to tell me about Brenda. I wonder where he is now. Probably at the restaurant, cleaning up after a busy night and filling all the little salt and pepper shakers stamped with "El Ranchero." Or maybe he's sitting cross-legged on his bed, listening to music and drawing. I pull my phone out of my pocket.

I'm scared. I don't know what to do. Give me another chance. I want to be your M again.

The door opens, and a girl I sort of recognize from school comes out.

"Mind if I join you?" she asks.

"Go ahead." I scoot over to make room on the steps. I close my phone, leaving the text message unsent.

"I think we had biology together sophomore year," the girl says.

"You're Dana, right?"

"Close enough. It's Danielle."

"I'm still Marisa."

Danielle laughs and fishes a cigarette out of her back pocket. "Yeah, I remember you. You want a smoke?"

"Nah."

She flicks her lighter and cups her hand around it as she guides the flame up to the cigarette in her mouth. She smokes in silence for a while.

"You look like you needed a break from the madness."

"I guess so." I shrug.

"First time I seen you at a party, isn't it?"

"Yeah, it's not really my scene."

"Really?"

"Usually I'm working. And there's stuff for school, you know how it is."

"I haven't been that dedicated this year, to be honest. But I been promising my boyfriend I'm going to get serious. He said he doesn't want to marry a dummy, so I'd better graduate. But you stuck with it, huh? I heard you were going to U of H."

"Yeah, maybe. I want to go somewhere."

Danielle exhales two streams of smoke from her nostrils and then turns my way. "Hey, totally different subject, but you hang out with Brenda Zepeda, right?"

"Yeah, sure. We came together tonight."

"So what's the deal with her and that white guy? Did they break up? Because I could swear I saw her making out with Pedro Jimenez."

I'm already standing up and opening the door. "Where did you see them?"

Danielle lowers her cigarette, surprised. "Just out with everybody else dancing. You OK?"

"I don't know," I say. "Nice talking to you." And I'm pushing my way back into the living room.

I look all over for Brenda, but I can't see her anywhere. I don't see Pedro, either. *Shit, oh shit.*

"Have you seen Brenda Zepeda?" I ask the guy working the stereo. I have to shout the question twice before he hears me.

"Hot chick in the black skirt?"

"Yes!" I holler.

"I think she went out to the garage to help mix up some more trash can punch."

At that moment, I catch sight of Pedro dancing with a skinny sophomore. So they aren't off alone somewhere. Thank God.

I'm going to go find Brenda and make her listen. I have to. But first, I need a chance to think. And some water. The drink Brenda gave me left this sickly sweet taste at the back of my throat. I walk to the drink table and look for a bottle of water, but I don't find anything. I snag a cup and work my way back to the kitchen.

Two freshmen girls are walking out as I come in, and they just giggle like idiots when they bump into me.

I turn on the faucet and watch the water run into the sink for a long time before I fill up the cup. I thought I was doing better, that I had everything under control, but now I feel like I'm going to puke. Scared, sick, and lost, just like that day in Ceci's bathroom.

Just then the kitchen door swings open and then slams shut. I spin around, and the water in the cup sloshes onto the floor.

It's Pedro. He's inches from me.

chapter 31

I can smell the booze on him and see it loosening things behind his eyes.

"Stop telling Brenda lies about me," Pedro says into my ear. "You don't want me to start talking about you, telling everyone *la verdad*, how you practically threw yourself at me. Your life is your business. My life is my business."

"No." I try to pull my arm free. "Brenda just doesn't know how you are, she . . ." I suck in a breath, determined not to cry. "You can't just do whatever you want with people, *a lo menos*, not with Brenda."

"How do you know what Brenda wants?" he sneers. "You don't even know what you want, *pendeja*. So just keep your stupid mouth shut."

I start for the door, but he grabs my wrist. "I'm not done talking to you."

This is not good.

He has a beer in his free hand, and he lifts it to his lips, draining it.

"*¡Suéltame!* You're hurting me," I say. I'm shaking.

"Shut up, you little tease." He squeezes my arm harder, twisting it back until I cry out.

"I told you to stop. That day, I told you I didn't want to," I say with as much force as I've got.

"Oh, come on. Your body was saying, 'Give it to me hard, *papi.*' " He points the beer bottle down and thrusts it at me. When he does it again, I grab it from him with my free hand. He laughs, but he doesn't try to take it back.

Instead, he lets go of my wrist and reaches around to grab my butt with both of his hands, pulling me in against him rough. "You're not fooling anybody. That day, you were begging for me to give it to you."

I squeeze the bottle tight.

"I told you no, you . . ."

"I what?" Pedro's mouth twists into a grimace. He raises his eyebrows, mocking me.

"Stop touching me!" I throw my elbows against him and he lets go for a minute, takes a step back.

He looks me up and down, then starts laughing. "You think you're hot stuff, huh? What a fucking joke. *Pura broma.* You're just a little girl, a little slut."

I know I should run now that Pedro's hands are off of me, but I don't. Because my head is swimming, and it's like the poison he put in my life that day at Ceci's is coming back all at once. I feel him on top of me again, see his lips twist into that nasty smile. My head is hanging over the toilet, Anita is crying, I'm alone, alone, alone with what I let happen.

And then I remember his arm around Brenda's shoulder.

My fear turns to rage so fast that I can't hold it back. I slam the bottle against the edge of the counter. The bottom half of the bottle shatters, leaving a jagged edge. Pedro stops laughing and just stares at me.

I grip the neck of the bottle tight and press toward him. "You were going to force me," I whisper just loud enough for him to hear. "I didn't want to, I told you no. You almost—you almost raped me." I point the broken bottle at him.

"You *pendeja* cunt," he says, shaking his head. But he takes a step back. Then another.

"You may think I'm just some stupid girl, *pero* I will so slice you open if you try to touch me again." I lean forward until the sharp edge of the bottle is pressed against his stomach. "The same goes for Brenda. Stay away." I hear myself speaking in a voice too calm and level to be mine.

"What the hell?" He tries to back up, but he's already against the wall. "Psycho bitch," he says, but his voice trembles just enough for me to know he's scared.

I jerk my arm to the right, grazing his arm with the broken glass.

"Fuck!" he shouts. A trail of red droplets beads up on his arm.

"You should leave."

"Hell no, this is my party—"

"Leave. Now." I think for a second about how I could hurt him the most, and I lower the bottle until it's close to his crotch. No matter how he moves, I can cut him now if I want to. I can cut him before he could grab my hand and stop me.

"Jesus fucking Christ! You are one fucked-up *pendeja*." He tries to sound tough, but his words fall flat.

I just stare at him with a calm I don't feel and hold the bottle steady. "*Vete*," I say again. "Go."

A second later he's out of the kitchen and shoving through the crowded living room. I watch as a few guys try to pull him into a drinking game, but he pushes them away and keeps moving.

The door to the garage opens just as he goes by, and Brenda walks in with a bucket of punch. She calls to him, but he shakes his head and pushes on toward the front door. A confused look passes over Brenda's face, then she shrugs and starts passing out drinks.

I'm OK. It's all OK. He's gone. I step back into the kitchen and look around me. There's a narrow door on the other side of the room, and I push it open. It's the laundry room. I step in and slide down against the dryer. Something is tumbling inside it. Suddenly I'm exhausted, and I just listen to the steady *thud-thud-woosh*. Right now, I don't need to think.

The dryer is still running when the door opens and a light flickers on. I blink against the sudden brightness.

"You OK?" Brenda asks. She squats down beside me. "Took me a while to find you. Too much booze, huh?" She holds her hand against my forehead. "No fever. Do you need—"

"Pedro tried to force me." I say it like ripping off a Band-Aid—the faster the better.

"What?" Brenda stares at me. "Bullshit. Don't joke about that; I saw him leave like an hour ago."

"Not tonight. Back at the end of March, right after the fight with my dad and everything with Alan. Pedro . . . I was at Cecilia's and he . . ."

Brenda puts her hand over her mouth. "Oh my God, Marisa. Oh, shit. All this time you were trying to tell me, and I just gave you hell. *Lo siento tanto*, babe." She drops all the way down to the floor and puts her hands on my knees. "I am so, so sorry," she says again. "Tell me what happened."

"So he came to see Jose, but Jose was at the doctor's. I was so lonely that when Pedro started talking to me, I felt a little better, and I talked to him." I look at Brenda, afraid that I'll see anger on her face, or even worse, blame. But she just reaches over to smooth my hair.

I tell her how he kissed me, how it felt good at first. How I knew it was wrong, but I just didn't want to think about Alan. How I wanted to feel free from everything.

"Everybody feels that way sometimes," she says.

When I finish telling her the rest, Brenda hugs me for a long time.

"Nobody should ever have to go through that," she says. "Especially not alone."

I look down. I'm still holding the broken beer bottle. I start to shake, half laughing, half crying again. "I was in here getting water, and he came in. Started talking shit, put his hands on me. I kind of snapped. I broke this, and then I pointed it at his balls and told him I'd cut him if he even thought about touching me. Or you."

"So that's why he was looking like a scared-shitless dog when he passed me. I could tell he was guilty for something, the *pendejo*." Brenda starts laughing too, and she leans back against the dryer next to me. "You got guts, *loca*, you know it?"

chapter 32

We're on our way to pick up Anita after school a few days later when Brenda's cell phone rings. She grabs it from the dashboard, then raises an eyebrow at me.

"It's Alan."

"Really?" I try to keep the hope out of my voice.

"Should I answer?"

"Of course, *mensa!*" For a second I forget she's driving and grab her arm.

"OK, OK!" She swats my hand away, then flips the phone open. "Hey, Alan. What's up?" She listens. "Really? What time did she start the labor and everything? Already? I love the name. Good for her. Sure, I'll tell her. Yeah, just give me the room number. OK . . . OK . . . See you soon."

"Jessica had her baby?"

"Three weeks early, but everything is fine. It's a girl. Katalina Cinthia Peralta. He wanted to know if we could bring flowers or something."

"We?"

"He asked me to tell you. You're coming, right?" Brenda says.

"Are you kidding? If he wants me there, nothing could keep me back."

Her cell rings again. This time it's Greg. "Looks like you and me both might get our chance," she says. "Time for some relationship CPR, *chica.*"

I watch Alan from where I'm standing at the end of a long hall in the hospital. He's the only one standing in front of a big window into some kind of hospital room. He seems so at peace that I'm afraid to disturb him.

"Hi," I say when I finally walk up beside him. "Your mom told me you'd be here. You should see the mess of balloons Brenda picked out. They barely fit through the door."

"Just look at her," he says reverently, pointing at a skinny, red-faced baby wearing nothing but a diaper. "Meet Katalina Cinthia Peralta." The baby is lying in a little plastic cart while a nurse cleans her foot.

"Wow," I say. To me she looks sort of like an alien monkey. But Alan is in a trance.

"So totally new," he murmurs.

"Yeah," I say. We watch as the nurse pulls out a needle and starts drawing blood from the baby's heel. "Is that normal?" I ask him.

Alan nods. "Jess asked me to come watch while they did the tests and stuff. She wanted somebody to stay with the baby until they bring her back to the room."

The nurse is done drawing the blood, and Katalina looks only a little pissed. I stare at her hard and try to see her through Alan's eyes. I want to slide in front of him, pull his arms around me, and listen to him tell me what he sees. Maybe it's just being close to him, but I can feel something I haven't felt in a long time creeping back into me. Hope.

There's a lot of truth that needs telling, ugly truth. And there are no guarantees. But the only chances I'm going to have are the ones I make for myself.

We stand there without talking for a long time, just watching Katalina as the nurse listens to her heart and does some other tests. Katalina purses her lips and sucks at the air, then presses her tiny fists against her cheeks. Her eyebrows wrinkle into twin squiggles when she starts to cry.

Alan doesn't take his eyes off of her. "Good strong lungs."

I don't know for sure, but I think there's an opening here, maybe just big enough for me to get through.

I slip my hand into his. He doesn't pull away.

chapter 33

"Are you nuts?" Cecilia says. Some of the people standing by us turn to stare.

"It's not like it's a crime for me to skip it, Ceci. Graduation is way more important. I don't even like to dress up." I elbow her so she'll move forward in the line. The department store is going out of business, so the place is packed. The checkout line is so long it looks like half of Houston is here.

"Your prom is a once-in-a-lifetime thing! You'll always regret it if you don't go. I mean, I thought about skipping it. I already had a big belly and everything. But for that one night, every girl is a princess, every guy is a prince."

"At least until the after-parties start," I say.

"Skip those, whatever. But the actual prom—the dancing, the fancy dresses, the pictures—you have to go. Doesn't Alan want to?"

I pull Anita back from the toys and candy that the evil store owners put right by the checkout. "He said it was up to me. But I don't want to spend that kind of money on a dress."

"It always comes back to money for us, doesn't it?" She sighs.

We finally make it to the front of the line, and Cecilia heaps up the clothes we picked out for Anita.

"These are 75 percent off?" Cecilia asks as she adds a pair of pink sandals to the pile.

"Everything's on clearance, hon," the saleswoman says. "They want this place emptied out by next Saturday so the new store can come in."

When she finishes paying, Ceci turns to me with this sneaky smile. "I want to look at one more thing," she says.

"After waiting in that long line, *now* you want to look at more stuff?" I shake my head. "Anita, your mama is crazy."

Anita twirls her finger in circles by her ear and chants, "*Loca, loca, loca!*"

Cecilia ignores us. "What's your hurry? You've got an hour before you have to be at work. Come on."

"Tía, *mira esto.*" Anita tugs on my arm and drags me over to another rack.

"Sweetheart, dresses have to be the right size. You can't just grab one and—" I shut up when I see it. It's strapless, with gauzy layers of shimmery material over soft gold

203

satin. A velvet ribbon wraps around just above the waist-line, and the skirt is full and elegant without being poofy. I'm not the kind of girl who dreams about prom dresses, but if I were, this is the dress I would want.

Anita's little feet peek out from inside the rack of dresses. She loves to hide there. Normally I'd be chasing her out, telling her that the rack could fall over, but right now all I want to do is check the dress size.

"Doesn't my daughter have good taste?" Cecilia says.

"She does. And look, *híjole*, she even picked the right size."

"It's a sign," Cecilia says. "Why don't you go try it on?"

"There's no point if it's a hundred and ninety dollars or something," I say.

Cecilia reaches for the tangle of tags hanging from the dress and flips through until she finds the price. "Not anymore. Used to be two hundred sixty, now it's twenty-six bucks. That's insanely cheap. Hey, it'll be my graduation present to you if it fits."

"OK, OK," I say.

Ten minutes later, we're standing in the enormous checkout line for the second time.

chapter 34

The wine Greg's uncle gave us with dinner is only a faint hum in the back of my brain by the time the limo driver drops Greg, Brenda, Alan, and me off at the hotel on the night of the prom. All the fancy extras are thanks to Greg's family. My dad—well, his big contribution was just letting me go.

"Oh my God," Brenda whispers when we walk into the ballroom.

We pass under a huge arc of roses and a sign that says "An Evening in Paris." Tables covered in white are staggered around a big dance floor, and each one has a bowl of white flowers floating in water. In the back corner by the photographer there's a giant Eiffel Tower. Long strands of white lights hang from the ceiling. Everywhere people are laughing, smiling, and moving funny in their prom gear.

I watch guys I've known since middle school walk between the tables with their dates. These are boys who talk dirty in the hall and look at porn on their cell phones, but tonight they hold their girls by the arm and act almost like gentlemen.

We make our rounds through the ballroom, stopping to talk to everybody we know. We take so many pictures that my mouth starts to hurt from smiling.

The DJ puts on a fast song, and the mood on the dance floor heats up.

"I love this song!" Brenda shouts, and she and Greg take off.

"Let's go too," I say to Alan, laughing and jumping up and down.

We squeeze in between a group of girls dancing together and a guy doing his own wild thing solo. It takes me a while, but I finally find the rhythm. Alan's having a harder time.

"Let's go toward the middle, it's easier to move there," I shout.

The next two songs are fast and get us sweating more than I'd like. Finally there's a slow one. Alan looks relieved as he pulls me close.

"I'm glad to be here with you," he says into my ear.

"Me too," I say. "I missed you. So, so much."

He's still talking, saying something sweet, but I stop hearing him. Because all of a sudden I'm back on Ceci's couch feeling Pedro move against me. My heart starts to break all over for what I almost did.

I lean my head against Alan's shoulder and try to let the sound of his heartbeat and the words of the song calm me down.

The song fades out before I'm ready for it to. We hold each other and wait for the next song. Instead, the stage lights up, and the senior class sponsor takes the microphone. "Time to announce this year's prom court!"

We watch as she names the dukes and duchesses, the jesters, and the lords and ladies. There's the occasional boo from people who voted for someone else, but mostly everyone claps and cheers.

"And this year's prom king..."

"Tony Mendez!" someone yells, stirring up a ripple of laughter. Tony is one of the slow kids in the special education classes. He doesn't get the joke, and his mother has to tug him back when he starts to roll his wheelchair toward the stage. That makes my heart hurt, but I don't have long to think about it.

"The prom king this year is... Pedro Jimenez!"

My heart skips a beat as he jogs up to the stage and does a little dance. The girls toward the front whistle and cheer him on.

Of course it's Pedro. This is not really a surprise—everybody's been saying it was going to be him—but hearing his name still hits me in the gut. Brenda shoots me a just-say-the-word-and-we-can-jump-his-ass look. I just shake my head and look down.

"You OK?" Alan asks softly. He squeezes my hand. Because even after everything I told him, he is still that good.

"Yeah, but let's get out of here for a while," I manage.

———

We slip out past the teachers and security guards at the door to the ballroom. I don't say anything because there are people milling all around us. There's a bunch of elevators, and as we walk past, one opens. I duck in, pulling Alan with me. We're the only ones inside, so I press the button for the highest floor. When I look over at him, I see that his face is red. His hand is hot in mine, too. He's pissed. I'm just hoping he's not pissed at me.

"I'm sorry, Alan," I say. "I mean, it's always somebody like Pedro who wins. Please don't let him ruin this night for us. He's not worth it."

"He's worth an ass-kicking, that's what he's worth." Alan lets go of my hand and paces the elevator. He looks like he'd like to take a bat to the wood paneling and punch through the pretty framed mirrors on the walls, but after a minute he takes a huge breath and comes back to stand next to me. We ride the rest of the way up in silence.

When we get off at the top floor, we're in another elevator lobby. This one has a glass door off to the side, and when I push it open a little, I'm surprised to feel outside air rush in to meet me.

Through the glass I can see a patio with a garden and a little stream. A path twists between big beds of red and yellow flowers. It's beautiful—magical, even.

"I guess this is supposed to be closed," he says, pushing a stack of folded lounge chairs out of the way of the door. "But it's open for us."

We walk along the dark path until we get to a little bridge, then we stop to watch the fish swim in their illuminated pond. They're orange, black, yellow, and silver. Whiskered, too. Like the ones you see in Chinese restaurant paintings.

Alan squeezes my hand. "Sorry for getting mad. I know we're putting this whole thing behind us, but it's not easy. He took advantage—"

I put a finger over his lips. "Yeah, he did, but I messed up before that."

Alan nips at my finger with his teeth and shrugs. "At least there's just a week of school left. Hopefully you'll never see his sorry skin again. He's probably not going to college. Or even if he does, he definitely won't be at U of H. The loser skips all his classes."

I feel my mouth go dry. It took all my guts to tell Alan about what happened with Pedro—and then to keep him from enlisting all his male relatives to pound Pedro into bits. Getting Alan to look me in the eye again, that took some time. Plus we've been busy visiting Jessica and Katalina and taking care of Anita.

So I haven't exactly had a ton of chances to say anything about the letter from UT or what Ms. Ford found out from her phone calls. But now I know I've got to, fairy tale night or not.

"What if I went somewhere besides U of H?"

"Like community college with Brenda? I mean, that's cool, but U of H is better, isn't it? For academics and all?"

"I mean, like somewhere in another city."

"What?" He looks up at me, and I think I see fear in his eyes, a fear I can understand. The fear that everything could be pulled out from under you at any moment.

"Ms. Ford says UT–Austin has the best engineering program in Texas."

"But you never applied to UT."

I lean back against the bridge railing and smooth my hands over my dress. "Yeah, I did," I manage to say.

"Shit, Marisa. And you didn't tell me?" The look on his face takes me back to the day under the oak tree. I shiver.

"I didn't know how, I . . ."

He's gripping the guardrail of the bridge so tight that his knuckles look white.

"So, at first I just applied because Ms. Ford was bugging me about it, and then . . ."

He doesn't say anything, so I tell him the whole story.

"Your mom hid the letter?" He slaps his hands against the railings. "Mexican mamas don't want their girls going away, that's for sure."

"Ms. Ford said that the dean of the engineering school was interested in my situation. They'll still let me in. He thinks there should be more girls like me in engineering, whatever that means. They even want to give me an extra scholarship." I look up at Alan and then back down at my hands. "So in a weird way, my mom's sneaking around could actually help me out. I mean, if I go."

"Just give me a sec, OK? Just a sec." He walks away from the bridge and walks around the garden. It seemed big enough when we first came out here, but I can tell he's wishing for a field, for space. For room to get away from me.

I turn back to watch the fish and ask myself why the hell I had to open my big mouth. But I already know why. Because I can't be with him and keep secrets between us, not after what we've already been through. Not after he forgave me.

When he finally comes back, he doesn't say anything, but he slides his hands around my waist and lifts me up until I'm sitting on the bridge's railing.

"Careful!" I squeal. I pull up my dress a little and wrap my legs around his chest so I won't fall. He steadies me with his hands and lets me lean against him.

"You've given me a lot of big news," he says softly. "Maybe too much."

"You have a right to be mad, I know it," I say.

"So it's off to UT, then." He doesn't look at me, but I can see how he's clenching his jaw.

"No," I say. The distance in his voice scares me. "I mean, I haven't decided anything. I've still got U of H."

"You're going to go. You want to be somebody, Marisa. You deserve to go to the best school. It's pretty obvious what's going to happen."

"You're mad."

"I just can't figure you out. I thought I had you back, and now I have to lose you all over again."

"You don't have to. I can be somebody right here."

"Think about it. In Austin, you could leave your books out whenever you want, no dirty looks from your dad." He lifts one hand to my cheek.

"I don't know what will happen with my parents if I go. And there's Anita."

"You can't stay behind forever trying to fix Cecilia's life. She'll find a way to manage. She's not perfect, but she loves her kid."

"Anita won't understand."

"Come on, Marisa. Do you want to go?"

"I think so."

"Then go. After everything that's happened, what anybody else wants doesn't really matter." He starts to lift me down from the railing.

"What about us?"

"That's how things go," he says, still not looking me in the eye. "Nothing ever stays the same."

"Alan." I put my hands around his neck and pull his face toward me. "If I go, it doesn't mean that I don't care. I don't want to lose you."

Finally he looks at me, and so many things seem to pass over his face that my heart starts to race. Now I'm going to have to pay for my mistakes; I just know it.

"Please," I say. "You could help me do this."

His eyes look wet, and he strokes my birthmark with his finger. I don't care if he rubs all the makeup off and our prom picture comes out bad. I just want to feel that touch as long as I can.

It seems like forever before he speaks.

"I know the way to Austin," he says so softly I can barely hear him.

"Thank you," I whisper.

His hand on my cheek slips down to my mouth. His fingertips graze my lips, and I'm still a little scared because I don't want Pedro to be anywhere inside our kiss. Alan just watches me and waits; he won't do anything till he knows that I'm OK with it. That's the kind of guy he is.

"Please," I say, "I want to kiss you back."

June

chapter 35

"Marisa, they're calling for us!" Brenda shouts before running back out of the bathroom. I dry my hands and straighten my gown. Not even the stupid graduation cap can bother me today.

The processional music starts up a second after I slip into line with the rest of my homeroom. I squint up into the stands as we march down the center aisle toward the stage, but I don't see my family.

Alan is just a few people ahead of me, and it makes me happy to see his messy brown hair sticking out from under his cap. He never turns around, just keeps moving forward.

The ceremony is long and boring except for the two minutes it takes you to walk up to the stage, cross it, and get your diploma. When the whole thing is over, we scream our class year and throw our graduation caps up in the air.

The caps spin and swerve like a flock of crows on their way back down, and I'm pretty sure the one I catch isn't the one I threw, but it doesn't matter. Today I feel like the whole world is mine.

There's lots of hugging and good-byes. I dodge questions about the future and fudge the truth when anyone presses for details.

Brenda overhears and shakes a finger at me. "If I wasn't so happy today, I'd be mad at you. Cutting out on me like this."

"Come on, Brenda," I grin. "You know you love me."

"I don't have a choice, do I? Nah, I'm not mad no more." She pulls me in for a hug. "We did it, *chica*. From dumpy middle-school kids to high-school graduates."

Then she spots her family.

"Over here, Ma!" she shouts, waving at her parents. Her dad's bald head is shiny with sweat, and his face glows with pride. "Go Brenda, go Brenda, go B-R-E-N-D-AAAAAA!" he chants. I walk over with her and hug her parents.

Alan comes over with his family and a bunch of relatives. I stay and talk, but mainly I'm looking for some sign of my own family.

"Want to hold her?" Jessica asks, tilting Katalina toward me.

"Sure." I take Katalina and support her head carefully. She stretches, yawns, and wiggles her legs a little. Then she kisses the air and makes a sucking sound.

"Uh-oh, she thinks it's dinnertime," I laugh.

"She's just happy when you hold her," Jessica says.

"You getting any rest?"

"She's a good sleeper, thank God." Jessica's eyes are tired, but she looks happy.

"*Tienes sueño*, little one?" I say. Katalina smiles up at me and puts her hand in her mouth.

"She won't be little for long. By the time I cross this stage, she's going to be running circles around me," Jessica says, gently lifting her baby from my arms.

"The important thing is that you get across the stage," Alan says, wrapping a protective arm around his sister.

Jessica nods, but she's not really listening. She's caught up in her baby again, stroking her tiny hands and talking to her in that secret language only mothers and their babies know.

That's when I finally catch sight of my family. Cecilia and Mami are carrying a homemade banner that says "CONGRATS MARISA!" and Anita runs toward me as soon as she sees me.

"Tía!" she shouts.

"Hi, beautiful," I say, scooping her up. "Did you get bored sitting up there for so long?"

"Nope, I got my books." She points to a bag looped over Cecilia's arm. "Abuelo let me read to him."

"Really?" I raise an eyebrow and set her back down. I can see my dad walking over with everyone else, arms folded over his chest. "That's a big deal. I tried to get your abuelo to read with me a long, long time ago, but he wouldn't."

"*Mira* what me and Mommy and Abue made for you!" She points at the banner and drags me through the crowd toward it.

"I'm coming, I'm coming! *Cuidado!*"

Anita nearly knocks over someone's grandmother and stops just short of crashing into Mami. Cecilia swats her on the bottom. "Manners!" she says.

"I'm so proud of you, *mija*," my mom says, squeezing me tight. "You have done a big thing." She holds my face between her hands and kisses my forehead. "I knew you would make it."

"Thank you, Mami. I love the banner; it's so pretty."

Cecilia jostles my mom's arm. "Come on, let me have a turn, Ma." She hands Anita the banner and smothers me in a hug. Gustavo doesn't wait for his turn; he just picks me up and swings me from side to side like he does with Anita. "You did it right, sis!"

"Put me down!" I shriek, digging my nails into his arms. He cracks up and plops me back down.

"Thank you," I say with as much dignity as I can manage. I scoop up my cap from the ground.

"I'm going to start looking for a good car for you, something to get you to U of H and back every day." Gustavo slaps my back hard.

"Great," I say weakly.

"*Mija*." Papi steps forward. I hesitate for a second, but when I kiss his cheek, I don't smell anything but the Old Spice cologne he always puts on for special occasions. "*Felicitaciones*," he says. "*Felicitaciones*, Marisa."

That's all he says, but when I search his face, I think I see a glimmer of pride. No matter what, he's still my dad.

"So what are we going to eat? All that sitting wore me out." Gustavo rubs his belly.

"Can I braid these, Tía Marisa?" Anita interrupts. She tugs at the honor cords draped over my gown. So my grades didn't turn out as sucky as I thought they would. *Gracias a Dios* for extra credit.

"In a little bit." I shake the cords out of her fingers. Past a clump of cheerleaders posing for a picture, Ms. Ford is talking to some kids from my calculus class.

"Ma, I'm going to go say good-bye to one of my teachers," I say. "I'll be right back."

"Congratulations," Ms. Ford calls, hugging me as soon as I walk up. The other students go off with their families, and we're alone.

"This is a big day," Ms. Ford says. Her eyes are moist and a little red, but she's still smiling.

"Thanks to you, miss."

"You talked to your parents?"

"Not yet."

"But you're going to?"

"I just need to find the right time." I take Anita's idea and keep my hands busy braiding both ends of the honor cords.

"They're your parents. They deserve to be part of this kind of decision."

"It's just that they . . ."

"Even if you think they don't agree, they should know."

I nod, but I have no intention of telling them.

"Good. So everything is set with the School of Engineering. You need to go by the office next week to fill out papers for your work-study job. You'll also be able to plan out your classes for the fall and register for the summer session."

"Wow," I say. I still can't believe it's me she's talking about. It's all happening so fast—which is how I want it to be, I guess. Might as well start with summer school. Lots of freshmen do it, Ms. Ford told me. And the sooner I go, the less time I have to chicken out.

"Where are you going to stay, again?"

"One of those co-ops you showed me online. The College House."

"Then all that's left is your graduation present." Ms. Ford reaches into her purse and pulls out a rectangular package with an envelope taped on top. "Your family's waiting for you. Open it later, OK?"

"Thank you so much. Calculus saved me this year."

"Don't be a stranger." Ms. Ford hugs me one more time. "I expect to hear from you."

"I'll be in touch. For sure."

"And just remember, it's not going to feel like home until you make it home."

chapter 36

It's almost midnight by the time I finally sit down on my bed. I went to Brenda's graduation party with Alan, but now I have to get my head together and pack.

From under the bed I pull out my old red duffel bag and a suitcase I borrowed from Brenda. I circle the room slowly, trying to decide what to take. I stop in front of the dresser and pull down the pictures I taped to the mirror over the years. I put them in a neat pile on my bed with a bilingual Bible I got for confirmation and a copy of *To Kill a Mockingbird* I won in an eighth-grade spelling bee. I lift a stack of T-shirts from a drawer and set it into the suitcase.

Ms. Ford's present is still on my bed, too. You're supposed to open the card first, but no one's watching, so I rip into the package instead. It's a brand new calculator, the graphing kind we used in AP calc. I know it's dorky, but I think it's beautiful. Who knows, maybe I didn't even pass the AP exam. But then again, maybe I did. By the time I find out in July, I'll be a real college student. I'll be on my way no matter what.

I slip my thumb under the flap of the envelope. The front of the card has a woman making a giant victory sign with her arms. Inside, the message is simple:

Marisa,

I hope this comes in handy in your engineering courses. But even more, I wish for you loads of the blessings that can't be calculated. You'll be in my thoughts. Go UT Longhorns!

—Ms. F

I slide the card and package into the suitcase and pick up Paco. I straighten his teddy bear button eyes and smooth the bare places in his fur left behind from the times Cecilia and I played barbershop with him ages ago.

I think about packing him, then decide that it's time for Paco to officially belong to Anita. I know everybody's going to be mad at first, but Anita's the only one I'm really worried about. I don't want her to think I left her.

I pull shoes out from under the bed one pair at a time. I'm digging deep for a missing flip-flop when my hand brushes against the box where I save my letters and cards.

There are lots of drawings from Alan, notes from Brenda going all the way back to middle school, collages and coloring pages from Anita, birthday cards from my aunt in Mexico. There's also a stack of postcards that I got here and there over the years. I pick up one with a picture of a bluebonnet and turn it over. Then I lay all the postcards out in front of me in neat rows. Cactuses, paintings, parks, cartoons, one with a D.A.R.E. slogan. None of them used. I stare at them for a while. Then I dig for a pen and start writing.

Dear Anita,

I bet you are probably wondering why I'm not home to see you right now. Remember that book you read to me about jobs? I'm at college in Austin so that someday I can have the job I want. But I won't forget about you, *chiquita*. I've got a whole stack of postcards just like this one, and I'll send you something new to read every week.

Love, Tía Marisa

I'm finishing my message when there's a knock on my door. I jump up and shove my bags under the bed. Probably it's Gustavo wanting to tell me some dumb drinking story.

But when I open the door, it's my mom standing there in her nightgown.

"Everything OK, Ma?"

"I want to talk to you."

"OK," I say a little hesitantly, opening the door wider. Suddenly I notice how bare the mirror looks. I see the clothes heaped by the door, the empty hangers in the closet, the pile of postcards.

But Mami doesn't look around. She keeps her hands rigid against her sides and walks to the bed so slowly that it seems like with every step she's fighting the urge to turn around and walk back out.

I smooth the blanket and sit next to my mom on the edge of the bed. I pull my legs up and drag Paco into my lap. I play with his soft teddy-bear ears and keep quiet; I'm not going to risk giving anything away.

"*Mija*, listen. I know I haven't been fair to you. Especially not what I did with that letter. The thing is, I've always needed you. I couldn't—I can't imagine handling things without you. *Tu papá* . . . he isn't such a good man sometimes." Her eyes are already getting damp.

"Shhh," I say, stroking her back.

"It's no excuse, *mija*; I know that. The things he's said and done . . . sometimes I can't believe that I stand by him."

"You don't have to."

"I was never like you, so much confidence, so much brains. I was always *burra*, slow. But I have been lucky. I got you and your brother and sister. And you are all fine *hijos*."

"We want to make you proud."

I can't decide if I should wipe away the tears trickling down my mother's cheeks or just pretend I don't see them. It's a matter of what will embarrass her least.

"Your brother and sister, they never wanted to go outside of here or do anything different. But you—"

"I know, Ma. I made it hard."

She hushes me. "You were always special, curious, interested in everything. And smart. I never knew how to be the right mom for you."

"It's OK. You tried; I know you did." I reach up to wipe her tears away. There are too many for my fingers to catch, so I use the corner of my pillowcase. "You're just worn out after such a long day."

"Where are you going, *mija*?" she says suddenly.

"Where am I going?" I repeat, not knowing what else to say.

"You never do laundry on the weekends," she says in a rush. "But yesterday I think you washed every piece of clothing you have."

"Ma! It's just laundry, it's not—"

"I know, Marisa. Tell me where."

I rub my eyes and shake my head.

"Is it like Vero? Please say no."

"I'm not joining the army, Ma."

"When are you leaving?" She stares right at me, and I know that she knows.

"Tomorrow morning, early," I say.

She breaks out in fresh tears. "It will be so hard without you. I can do better for you here. Please, *mija*."

I set down my bear and reach for Mami's hands. "It's Austin, not Germany. Just three hours away."

She takes a deep breath, then lets it out. "I thought I could just keep you here, but no. I'll be right back." She stands up and walks slowly out of the room.

I'm afraid she's going to get Papi, but I'm too stunned to move.

She comes back in carrying a shopping bag. "I have to let you live the right life for you, *mija*. So this is for you." She pulls out a black overnight bag. "I know you need something bigger to move your things, but I thought maybe you could use this for when you come home to see us."

"It's beautiful, Mami. Thank you."

Then I set the bag aside and stroke my mom's hands while I try to take in what I just heard. Her skin is soft in places, calloused in others.

"*Mira*, tomorrow I'm going to pretend that I didn't know nothing about this." She holds me tight. "And if your father stays in the bedroom when you come home, *qué importa*? Not that different from how he is now."

"Ma?"

"*Sí, mija?*"

"Can you do a favor for me? I'm making something for Anita. A present, I guess. If I leave it here with Paco, will you make sure she gets it? And I want her to have him, too." I pat the bear's head and try not to cry.

She squeezes my hand. "*Por supuesto.*"

"This means everything to me, Mami. The bag, but even more what you said." I hug her again and try to pour every warm feeling I have into it. Maybe that way it will last until I can come home again. "You are the right kind of mom for me."

chapter 37

Alan grabs my bags and lifts them into the truck. There's a faint hum of insects, but otherwise the street is silent.

I stare at the house and hope that Papi won't take his anger out on Mami when he realizes I'm gone.

"Ready to do this?" Alan asks. It's too dark for me to see his face clearly, but I think that maybe he's giving me one last chance to change my mind.

I hesitate. I can still go to U of H and stay in Houston with him. I can see his drawings and hear about his art program and laugh with him and take Anita to the park. I can show Jessica how to hold Katalina when she gets colic and be there when she eats her first solid food. I can go to Mass with Mami and serve Papi his silent breakfasts. I can make it here. It could be a good enough life.

"I'm ready," I say. This is not just another day—it's my day.

Alan starts the truck. "OK, then."

I watch in the side-view mirror as my house shrinks and then finally disappears when we turn the corner.

Alan tells me to sleep, since I've been up all night packing. I mean to close my eyes for only a second, but when I open them, it's full morning and there are already signs for Austin. Alan's singing along with the radio.

"You're killing me," I say. I'm yawning and laughing at the same time.

"Do you remember choir freshman year?" he asks.

"Poor Mrs. Baxter! She tried so hard to be nice, but you, me, and Brenda, we made it really hard on her."

"I'll never forget the look on her face when she finally came to talk to us before the spring concert. 'You three,' she goes, 'you all just mouth the words.' I couldn't stop laughing. She still gave us A's, though. Crazy woman."

We fall silent, and I stare at the dry hill country outside the windows. I feel the dark feelings creeping into the empty space between us.

I roll down my window and stick my head and arms out. The warm air rushes over my skin. I tell myself not to cry. I tell myself to be happy. I can almost feel a real smile fighting off the fear.

All of a sudden I feel a bunch of tiny slaps on my cheek. I open my eyes in time to see a floating black cloud swirling around me. Black flecks buzz and ping against my face and arms. Two of the bugs land on my tongue.

I duck back into the truck and spit into my hand. By the time the window is up, Alan is nearly in tears.

"It's not funny," I say, but I'm laughing too. I wipe bug goo from my cheeks.

"Your face, oh man," he says. "I wish you could have seen it. You were all happy, basking in the sun like a little turtle, and then BAM, the lovebugs hit."

"Lovebugs?" I say. Then I see why they're called that. Because they're not flying solo. Each bug has its legs wrapped around another one. I guess holding on too tight to what you love can be dangerous.

"Fatal attraction," Alan says as half a dozen more pairs splatter on the windshield. "Hey, bug eater, check the directions. Is this our exit?"

We've already dragged my bags up two flights of stairs and into the room that's going to be mine here at the College House Co-op. Now we're standing by the window and trying to say good-bye.

"Well, here I am," I say, pressing my fingers against the glass. It's scorching hot, and I pull my hand back with a yelp.

"Silly girl," Alan says. He's right. It's June, and I've lived in Texas my whole life; I definitely should know better.

He blows on my injured hand and points out the window. "Look how close you are to campus." We can see the tops of the UT buildings, and all the people who pass on the sidewalks seem to be heading that way.

I try to imagine making that trip myself, or finding the engineering office, or registering for classes. I can't see myself eating at the house's long dining table or sleeping alone in this bedroom. I can't see any of it.

"I'm scared."

"You've still got me, OK?" Alan says.

"But—"

"You know me, all right? You *know* me."

"Yeah, I know you." He's a hundred times more real to me than UT. I don't even know a damn thing about engineering. I look away. "You'll just get busy, with art classes and work and helping Jessica with Katalina and—"

"I won't forget about you," he says.

I sit down on the droopy couch by the window and close my eyes against the tears. This is probably the thirtieth time I've cried in the past two weeks, and I'm thinking maybe he won't be that sad to be rid of me.

"Look at me," he says.

I force myself to open my eyes. He's sitting next to me, holding out a large blue jewelry box.

I must have a crazy look on my face, because Alan says, "Don't freak out on me. It's not *that*. Just open it."

I reach for the blue box and lift the lid. Inside there's a perfect origami butterfly. Its wings and body shimmer red, green, orange, and gold in the sunlight from the windows. I breathe out and it flutters, almost like a real butterfly.

"It's gorgeous," I whisper.

"Not finished." He pulls a rolled piece of paper from behind him. "Go ahead."

I tug off the blue ribbon and unroll the paper. I smooth it out against my thighs. The drawing is of Alan. There are his long eyelashes, his smile, his generous hands. From his heart there's another image blooming. Dozens of butterflies perch on blades of grass in a field. Just right of the center, one butterfly lifts its wings above the rest. It's red and orange and green and gold like the one he made for me.

"So that you don't forget me, either," he says.

I press my face into his shoulder. I want him to promise that our lives will weave together and be beautiful like his drawings. But I don't say it.

"Just keep being you," he says. He pulls my right hand into his lap and uses one of his Sharpies to draw a butterfly onto my palm. He traces it with his thumb, and I can still feel the outline of the butterfly when we say good-bye on the front steps a few minutes later.

If this were a fairy tale, I'd know right now that all my dark feelings will go away and that I'll make it here in Austin. I'd know that Alan will be a famous illustrator, that Jessica will go to college, that Anita will straighten out her parents and stop wetting her pants, that someday the cold thing inside my dad will melt.

But I don't know any of that, so I tape Alan's drawing up over my new bed, which isn't new at all and smells kind of like moldy carpet. I put my clothes away in the dresser. And when something scurries over my foot, I act without even thinking. I kill my first Austin cockroach and get bug guts all over my UT course catalog. It's gross, but it's also kind of appropriate because I haven't left the real world. There's no magic here, just my own life.

acknowledgments

I owe a great professional debt to my agent, Steven Chudney, and to my editor, Andrew Karre, both of whom have been gracious guides to this most cautious of travelers.

This book would not exist without the many remarkable students I taught at Chávez High School. They told me about the book they wanted to read, and I tried to write it. In particular, I'd like to thank those who commented on early drafts: Krystal Chávez, Diana Alvarez, Karina López, and Jessica van Ravenhorst. Although they are now "grown," the kids who had me for 10th, 11th, and 12th grades are still cracking jokes, doing SSR, practicing scholarly habits, and terrorizing the halls in my memories, especially Edith Barrón, Veronica Carbajal, Cínthia Carcamo, Baltazar Díaz, Pedro Galindo, Veronica García, Jonathan Guevara, Whitney Horton, Charlie Machado, Melissa Martínez, Rey Mejía, Alicia Perrett, Alejandra Quijada, Roxann Rodríguez, Kristy Solorio, Yuridia

Treviño, Eric Vitales, and Jarol Wadel. A special thank-you to the D-house boys, who read this book to the end and then told me that it was the first they'd ever finished. (Don't worry, J and M, I won't blow your cover.)

My gratitude also to Linda Sue Alsup and the Greater Houston Area Writing Project for teaching me to share my writing with students; to Jane Eixmann and the librarians of Houston ISD, the Houston Public Library, and beyond; to Laura Furman, John Trimble, Karen Joy Fowler, and the many other mentors who took my writing seriously; to the members of OWL and to all the readers whose feedback helped shape the novel; and to Alisa and Mushu for walking the writer's path with me every week.

Thank you to my El Paso family for telling stories and making tamales and pozole with chicken. Thank you to my Houston family, Sarah and Shelley, for a friendship that nourishes me and makes writing possible. Thank you to my mother, who has always told me, "It'll be a crime if you don't write a book"; my father, who has his eye peeled for a Pullet Surprise; and my brother, Justin, who never misses a thing. Thank you, Arnulfo: you are the one who keeps me running, writing, and living with a joyful heart. Liam Miguel, your smile writes its own books; thank you for giving Mami time to write hers.